T0158361

HUNTING FOR THE MISSISSIPPI

Camille Bouchard

HUNTING
FOR THE
MISSISSIPPI

Translated by Peter McCambridge

**Baraka
Books**

Montréal

Édition originale en langue française parue sous le titre *Le rôle des cochons*
© 2014, Éditions Québec-Amérique

Translation © 2016 Baraka Books

ISBN 978-1-77186-072-7 pbk; 978-1-77186-073-4 epub; 978-1-77186-074-1 pdf; 978-1-77186-075-8 mobi/pocket

Cover by Folio infographie
Cover Illustration by Vincent Partel
Back cover photo: courtesy of Barclay Gibson
Book design by Folio infographie

Legal Deposit, 2nd quarter 2016

Bibliothèque et Archives nationales du Québec
Library and Archives Canada

Published by Baraka Books of Montreal
6977, rue Lacroix
Montréal, Québec H4E 2V4
Telephone: 514 808-8504
info@barakabooks.com
www.barakabooks.com

Printed and bound in Quebec

We acknowledge the support from the Société de développement des entreprises culturelles (SODEC) and the Government of Quebec tax credit for book publishing administered by SODEC.

Société
de développement
des entreprises
culturelles
Québec

We acknowledge the support of the Canada Council for the Arts, which last year invested $153 million to bring the arts to Canadians throughout the country.

Financé par le gouvernement du Canada
Funded by the Government of Canada | Canadä

Trade Distribution & Returns
Canada and the United States
Independent Publishers Group
1-800-888-4741 (IPG1);
orders@ipgbook.com

TABLE OF CONTENTS

"In the name of Louis XIV, King of France and Navarre, on this, the 9th day of April, 1682, I, René-Robert Cavelier de La Salle, by virtue of His Majesty's commission, which I hold in my hands, and which may be seen by all whom it may concern, have taken and do now take, in the name of His Majesty and of his successors to the crown, possession of the country of Louisiana, the seas, harbours, ports, bays, adjacent straits, and all the nations, peoples, provinces, cities, towns, villages, mines, minerals, fisheries, streams, and rivers, within the extent of the said Louisiana."

Ceremony founding Louisiana,
a milestone in the history of New France

READER'S NOTE

This novel is based on fact. The violence and horrors experienced by the characters were the lot of many explorers of the time and were not dreamed up by my imagination.

The term "savage" should not be given the negative connotation it has today, and at the time the term simply meant "woodsman." However, the word "Indian" is bound to an historical mistake attributed to Spain's first colonizers. I have therefore avoided using the term, except in dialogue.

C. B.

PART I

La Rochelle, 1684

I

IT'S A TOUGH LIFE

My mom's been wearing the same dress for months. Come to think of it, she's been wearing it ever since the fever took my father. It's not her way of showing she's in mourning: it's because she has nothing else to wear. From time to time, at dusk or dawn, she undresses by the sea in the dark. She gives the dress a good scrub, before putting it back on, still wet. That's fine in summer, but in winter...

My little brother Armand is five years old. He and I prefer not to wash. We're covered in lice and fleas, but at least we don't freeze. And now my younger brother is coughing all the time. Sometimes he doesn't sleep at night. He's even started spitting up blood. So there's no way he's going to get his clothes wet either.

Poor and hungry, the three of us live in a hovel in La Rochelle, France.

In a big town like this, with no family or friends, a widow with two children has barely anyone to turn to. Unless she has a little money set aside.

Mom doesn't have a cent. She doesn't have any friends to speak of either.

From time to time, on the way out of mass, passersby hand us a crust of bread, a half-eaten piece of fruit, a handful of chestnuts, or if we're lucky, a coin. Armand and I sing to attract more sympathy. We sing badly, but we sing all the same. It doesn't bring in much, but now and again we're happy enough.

"Such lovely children!"

I hate adults running their hands through my hair like that. It's not so much what they do as why they're doing it that upsets me. No one thinks I'm twelve; everyone thinks I'm younger. Much younger. I'm not tall or stocky, not by a long shot. And that comes in handy for Mom as she looks to attract the sympathy of onlookers. But I can't stand looking like a little kid! I'm almost a man, for heaven's sake!

I cross myself quickly. I've just sworn outside the church.

"Aagh!"

The shriek comes from Mom, who is sitting on the ground. At first I think she's shrieking at the shiny copper coin the parish priest has just slipped into her palm. Then I see that the same priest, still leaning over my mother, has grabbed one of her breasts.

"If you're looking for more money, Delphine, leave the two kids here and come into the sacristy with me."

And the priest ruffles our hair before striding off toward the door at the side of the church. His long Franciscan robe whips up the filth of the street as he walks. The hem is stained with dust and dog poop.

My mother, still on the ground, looks at the coin, then at my brother, at me, at the coin, my brother... She seems to be thinking hard. She half turns toward the priest, who has disappeared into the church through the sacristy door.

Mom stays where she is, thinks things over a little more, then bursts into tears.

Life, for a widow, can be tough.

✍

"Hey, Stache. How's it going?"

My name's Eustache. Eustache Bréman. I don't really know why, but Marie-Élisabeth Talon has taken to calling me "Stache." In different circumstances I think that would drive me mad. But I'll forgive Marie-Élisabeth Talon anything.

Anything at all.

"Wanna go draw on the beach with Armand, Jean-Baptiste, and Ludovic?"

She always treats me like I haven't even already turned ten or, worse, as though I was the same age as Pierre, her brother, who's two years younger than her!

But I forgive her. Because of her blue eyes. Because they remind me of the sea around the Island of Ré. Because they remind me of blueberries in the summer sun. I also forgive her because of her thick, wavy hair and the long brown locks that frame her perfect face.

I hold nothing against Marie-Élisabeth Talon because I'm in love with her. Totally, irreparably, infinitely in love with her. She is ten years old and I am twelve. We are made for each other, I'm sure of it.

Aside from the fact that she has no idea.

"Did you see the big fish Jean-Baptiste drew? I'm sure you could do better."

Curse this scrawny little body of mine! Curse my body of a child! I have the mind of an adult.

"I'm twelve, you know, Marie-Élisabeth. I have no time for playing with your brothers like little kids."

She frowns a little, but doesn't look at me. Instead she keeps an eye on the rabble of kids as they run around.

The Talons have five children. Marie-Élisabeth is the eldest. Then there's Pierre, who's eight. Then Jean-Baptiste, seven, Ludovic, five, and Madeleine, four. All with blueberry eyes. Like Mr. and Mrs. Talon.

"You look younger," she replies eventually. She's not being mean, just explaining why she thought I might like to play with the kids.

"I'm twelve. Old enough to be going out with you."

She laughs. Still doesn't look at me.

"I *want* to go out with you, Marie-Élisabeth."

She laughs. Still doesn't look at me.

My mom and Mrs. Talon are friends. They know each other, I mean. I don't know any longer if Mr. Talon was close to my dad, but the women say hello to each other when they meet, talk about women stuff, laugh over the occasional shared joke… One time Mrs. Talon even gave Mom a loaf of bread.

"Come on, Isabelle," my mom protested. "You have five kids. I can't accept this."

"But I have a husband, Delphine. Who works. We don't always eat our fill, but when God gives us a little more than we need, it's to help those worse off than ourselves."

Any food we manage to get is always for my little brother first. Mom and I make do with what's left over.

Or that's how it is until he dies. And the sad thing that day is that even though we get his portion, we don't have much of an appetite.

As we watch the gravedigger bury Armand, Mom holds me tight and cries. She cries really hard. And she holds me really tight. I should be the one consoling her, clutching her to my chest. My manly chest that looks like a child's. In Mom's eyes, I'm still a little boy. And I have to admit that as I watch my younger brother disappear into a big hole that is covered with lime, I feel very little.

Very little indeed.

2

THE FRUIT BENEATH
THE HOOF

"You can't imagine how huge the country is."

My heart is crushed like an over-ripe fruit beneath a horse's hoof.

"You can walk for weeks—weeks, Delphine!—without meeting a living soul. Nothing but forests and lakes filled with the purest water."

Mrs. Talon, her husband (his first name is Lucien), and my mom are sharing a watered-down cider bought on the cheap from a peddler. Their three youngest children are sleeping on the straw mattress they share as a bed. Pierre and Marie-Élisabeth are off in the corner, shelling dried peas they got who knows where. I'm standing next to my mom.

"It sounds heavenly," Mom replies, with a dreamy look that can be heard in her voice. "So much so... so much so that it seems impossible."

"It's not so simple, it's not that easy," Lucien Talon retorts. "You need to provide your own food, whether that means sowing seeds, picking berries, hunting, or fishing, and the

Savages are best avoided, but there's so much space... Life there..."

"So many animals, Delphine. Deer, hares, partridges... So many birds that they mask the sky like huge storm clouds. So many fish that you could walk across the waves." So many this... so many that...

As she reels off all the wonders, I think to myself that my love alone, no matter how intense, will never be enough to convince Marie-Élisabeth—let alone her parents!—to stay. To decide not to return to this America, where they have already lived, and whose marvels they are keen to share with us.

What will I do once the Talons are aboard the huge ship come to take them away? How will I bear to watch the setting sun, knowing that on the other side of the ocean it lights up the afternoons of the girl I love?

No longer an over-ripe fruit, my heart has become a dried pea that Marie-Élisabeth is shelling without a shred of emotion.

"Isn't there a terrible winter in this country of yours?" Mom asks, drumming her index finger on her bottom lip.

"Only in Canada," replies Mr. Talon, his irises resembling two big drops of blue sea water that have fallen into his eyes. "At Québec, where we got married, we'd never been so cold in our lives. But not in Louisiana. It hardly ever freezes there. At least, not like here, and much less than in Canada. Aside from a few winter nights, the weather there is mild and warm."

"And," his wife chips in, leaning over the table to take Mom's fingers in her own, "the king will shower all kinds of privileges on the first baby born in the colony. Titles, a seigneury..."

"A seigneury?" splutters my mother. "And you're planning on having another baby over there?"

Mrs. Talon steps back to rest her hands on her belly. "It's already on its way," she says, her voice barely a whisper.

I instinctively turn to Marie-Élisabeth and Pierre. Do they know they will soon have a new little brother or sister?

Either they didn't hear or they already know because they don't react. When I look back at my mother, even from my angle, I can see her jaw drop.

"You're expecting?" she finally manages, pronouncing each syllable slowly.

"We've counted the days," Lucien Talon replies, "and if the crossing isn't delayed, our child will be born in Louisiana."

The man clutches his wife's hand and holds it for a moment. The four drops of seawater of their irises blend together in a display of everlasting love. So much love, in fact, that my heart is torn a little more.

I no longer dare turn to face Marie-Élisabeth and I don't feel like exchanging glances with my mom either. Mom is staring at me now, but I know it's less about looking at me and more about averting her gaze from the couple. Because she still misses Dad. Like I will miss Marie-Élisabeth.

"Why don't you come, too?"

It takes a long while for me to get my head around Isabelle Talon's question to my mom.

"To... America?" she stammers after a moment's hesitation.

"Of course!" says Mr. Talon. "The leader of the expedition—"

He breaks off. "It will be René-Robert Cavelier de La Salle. His Majesty has just appointed him governor of Louisiana. And Mr. De La Salle will be only too glad to see you. Of the three hundred people set to go on the expedition, there are only a handful of women. How will we ever establish a colony worthy of the name if there aren't enough women for the men who wish to stay and start a family?"

"But I'm a widow!"

"Precisely, Delphine!" says Lucien Talon enthusiastically. "You are free to take a second husband. A new father for Eustache, you'll have some more children, replace the one you... I mean, the one who..."

"You'll be able to eat every day," Isabelle Talon interrupts before her husband mentions Armand. Every time Mom hears his name she bursts into tears. "It's not like here, Delphine. You won't have to go begging for bread. You'll be able to bake your own, and who knows, maybe bread for the rest of the village."

Mom bursts out laughing as though she's just heard the best joke ever.

"Come off it!" she gasps. "Can you really see me with... with another husband?"

"Why ever not?" retorts Lucien Talon, turning serious. "You're still young, Delphine, and—if I may—a very beautiful woman. The men on the expedition will be falling over each other to have your hand. The paradise we've been telling you all about can be yours too."

I feel a sharp pain coming from the knuckles on my right hand. Mom has grabbed hold of my fingers without realizing just how hard she is squeezing. It's less as though she's considering the offer and more like she's holding on to a mast or rope to keep her feet.

My heart—my flat, saddened heart—swells when I notice Marie-Élisabeth staring over at me. Like she's trying to read my mind, to find out if I'd like to go with them. Or to mentally sway the decision that is Mom's to make.

Intimidated, I look back at my mom. I almost jump when I see how she's looking at me.

"Eustache…"

"Mo… Mom?"

"Would you be scared of going on a big—a very big—ship?"

I mull over the answer in my head, but try as I might I can't put into words just how strong my desire is to leave with Marie-Élisabeth Talon. My heart is now as strong as a horse's hoof crushing a ripe fruit underfoot.

3

GOING ON A BIG—
A VERY BIG—SHIP

The first time I set eyes on Mr. René-Robert Cavelier de La Salle, we are already on the quay. We're getting ready to board the ships chartered for the expedition. He is very busy as he approves every detail the captains, quartermasters, clerks, and officers bring to his attention. Documents are brought to him, and approved with a brusque nod; gentlemen and priests are introduced to him, and greeted with a brusque nod; and various things on the boats are pointed out to him, and approved or turned down with a brusque nod or shake of the head.

He is wearing a broad hat with a white feather, which shakes precariously with every nod of approval.

De La Salle is at least forty years old. He is of average size, but his proud manner and the authority emanating from him make him seem taller to me. I am very impressed. If ever he deigned to look down at me, you can be sure I would look away.

Mom can't stop staring at him. I'm surprised because I've never caught her showing any interest in a man before. It's fun to try to figure out what she finds most attractive: his tiny chin with a discreet dimple at its centre? His fleshy mouth? His nose that sticks out? His blue-green eyes that seem to take in every detail of the bustling wharfs? (Eyes that bulge a little, if you ask me.) His long curly hair, a wig just as in court?

"And him?"

My mom looks away from Cavelier de La Salle to answer the great bear of a man signing up the volunteers on a makeshift trestle table.

"Eustache Bréman."

The secretary's black beard covers his whole face and runs so far down his chest that it gets lost somewhere in the middle of his open shirt. He has enough body hair to make men of five boys like me.

"How old is he?"

"Twelve," says my mother before I can open my mouth.

The bear looks me up and down, one huge eyebrow hoisted above the other.

"The kid barely looks eight."

"And I'm telling you he's twelve," my mom retorts, sounding irritated. "I should know! I spent thirty hours giving birth to him."

"That's fine, little lady. No need to get all worked up."

He mutters to himself while he writes down my details. "As if I care whether he's eight or twelve or twenty…"

Clearly this bear with a sore head doesn't just look like a bear.

Beside us, Lucien Talon and his two oldest sons—Pierre and Jean-Baptiste—are bringing over a trunk. It doesn't seem particularly heavy.

"That's everything we have, Stache," Marie-Élisabeth tells me proudly, pointing at it with her little white finger. "It's a lot to carry, isn't it? But there are seven of us."

I bite my tongue. I've already seen Mr. De La Salle's officers and first mates with four or five heavier trunks each. Mom and I are happy enough to be carrying a bag on our backs, bags into which we have fastened the few possessions we have. For me: a spare pair of pants (too short), two odd shoes (that might still come in handy someday), a pocket knife whose blade is broken (in the middle), a handkerchief with a hole in it (something to remember my little brother by), a terracotta bowl whose sides are so beaten up that I often have to hold it at an angle so as not to spill its contents. For Mom: a worn-out skirt given her by Mrs. Talon, a man's shirt that has come unstitched given her by Mr. Talon, the spoils of the last few times we went begging in La Rochelle, a scrap from a mantilla scarf that has become a handkerchief, a wooden comb made by my father (the only keepsake she has of his), and a cherrywood rabbit that looks like a dog turd big enough to hold in one hand, sculpted by Armand back when he would play with my pocket knife (the only thing she has to remember him by).

"So, my boy? Ready for the big adventure?"

I give a start.

Mr. Cavelier de La Salle's heavy hand is on my shoulder. I scramble for a brilliant reply, but by the time I come up with anything our leader is busy talking to Mr. Talon.

"Good to see you again, Lucien. And to see that your courage has not waned."

"I wouldn't have missed it for the world, sir."

The first mates surround the expedition leader, saying hello, left and right. Members of the Cavelier family are there, among them a priest who is our leader's brother and a soldier who is his nephew.

"And you, Mrs. Talon," De La Salle continues, bowing slightly. "Your beauty and audacity are an example for all. The sea holds no fears for you, by the look of things."

"No more than the ten other women on the mission, sir," coos Mrs. Talon. She gives what to me looks like an awkward curtsey but, well, what do I know? "In fact, one of them is my good friend: Mrs. Delphine Bréman, a widow, if I may introduce her."

De La Salle removes his hat before my mom, exposing the powdered locks of his wig to the sun and the wind.

"I bow down before the wonderful spirit of adventure that is alive and well in you, ma'am."

My mother turns bright red and gives a curtsey that is even more awkward than Mrs. Talon's. Both women are keen to bow and scrape before him, it seems.

I look to the side and see Marie-Élisabeth teaching Madeleine, the youngest at four years old, how to gently raise the bottom of her skirt and lower her head.

Four ships await our expedition, their yards bobbing up and down at the quays in La Rochelle. I try to commit their names and details to heart. I want to look as though I know what I'm talking about when I talk to the adults later.

First there's a huge warship with forty cannons—yes, forty!—under the orders of the captain of the navy, Tanguy Le Gallois de Beaujeu. He's a gruff, austere man, who doesn't seem at all nice, if you ask me. He has a way of loo-king at you that...

Anyway, back to the ships. The warship has a name that doesn't seem to fit at all: *Le Joly*. Although it is very beauti-ful, with its polished masts, gleaming deck, and scrubbed hull.

Next is the ship Mr. De La Salle will be boarding with the top brass: a three-master by the name of *La Belle*. It is smaller than the others and has few cannons. Then comes a three-hundred-ton supply ship with *L'Aimable* written large on its stern. Let's hope it lives up to its name and will bring us to our destination amiably enough.

And, to finish, a ketch—a ship with two masts, weighing I don't know how many tons, but smaller than the others—transporting all Mr. De La Salle's possessions (implements, tools, and other items required to establish the colony). Its name is the *Saint-François*.

The king himself—our beloved Louis XIV—provided *Le Joly* and *La Belle*. Mr. De La Salle rented the other two ships from French merchants. The king also supplied one hundred soldiers, the ships' crews, and skilled workers for the colony. But Mr. De La Salle must pay for the goods to trade with the Natives out of his own pocket.

That's all I've learned for the time being. We'll see what else I can find out.

On the morning of July 24, 1684, there are just under three hundred of us setting sail aboard the ships I have just described, including one hundred soldiers, artisans, six Recollect missionaries, and fewer than ten women with their children.

PART II

At Sea

4

WORK FOR PIGS

The sailors are used to the sea, the ships, and the strange rocking motion atop the waves. They don't bat an eyelid at the objects that are moving about, the people losing their balance, the creaking of the rigging, the wheezing of the ropes, the squeaking of the sails.

The same can't be said for us, the passengers aboard *L'Aimable*, nor for the hundred soldiers on board *Le Joly*. We need time to get used to these noises and movements before we can sleep, eat, or use the bathroom, perched above a hole in the ship's bow. Hats off to anyone who manages it without making a mess.

I also discover that among the travellers—and among the soldiers, I've heard the sailors say as they roar with laughter—many just can't bear the floor swaying beneath them. Some keep to the back of the hold, throwing up the little they manage to swallow. Once they get used to things after a few days, they are so thin that it's hard to look at.

And now the quarters where we live stink! They can barely walk—which means they do their business all around them. The wood is covered with vomit and excrement...

much to the delight of the pigs we have on board. Aside from pigs, we're also bringing chickens, sheep, turkeys, rabbits, and dogs with us. All of whom also relieve themselves where they lay. It drains away to the depths of the ship into a kind of gutter called the bilge. And that's not to mention the rats. No one invited them on board, but the ship is swarming with them, just like the lice on our heads.

All of which means that, weather permitting, my mom, the Talons, and I go out to the deck of *L'Aimable* every chance we get for some fresh air. Like just now, when, along with Pierre and Jean-Baptiste, Marie-Élisabeth and I are dozing off in the midday sun.

"Darnation and tarnation!"

Marie-Élisabeth cries out in pain as a passenger, who wasn't looking where he was going, walks right into her. He drops the leather bag he was carrying and then bumps into a pump lever. A new string of curses ensues, while the two men accompanying him rush to help.

"What in tarnation are these darned children doing on the expedition? And what are they doing on deck?"

Marie-Élisabeth moans as she rubs her ribs and picks herself up. I scramble to my feet as well, glancing over at Mr. Talon who is at the other railing with his wife and the younger children. Mom is at the head, where we go to the bathroom.

"You little cretin! Couldn't you loll around somewhere else than right in the middle of the passage?"

I don't like the look of him. Because he's insulting Marie-Élisabeth. He must be twenty-two, twenty-five.

"I've had lice bigger than you! Just stick close to the railing, idiot!"

He lifts his hand to strike Marie-Élisabeth. "Maybe this'll help you remember!"

In a fraction of a second I can see Mr. Talon stand up and get ready to come over, but he's too far away and too slow to prevent the angry man from striking his little girl.

I don't think. I've been playing with a piece of rope that has a pulley at one end. I don't take a run-up. I throw the whole thing as hard as I can, without bothering to aim. The wooden pulley—which is fairly heavy—hits the man on the shoulder just as his arm comes crashing down.

"Ouch! Why you little..."

Instinctively, he not only stops what he was doing, but half turns to protect his face. He brings his left hand to the spot where the pulley hit him. I don't think I really hurt him, but the element of surprise worked like a charm.

"The nasty little brat... the nasty little brat..."

He looks at me more in surprise than anger. Or for the first second at least, because it quickly gives way to a death stare. At least I've chalked up an initial success: he's turned his attention away from Marie-Élisabeth. Now I just need to come up with a second brilliant idea to escape his wrath.

As his companions hold the angry man back, Mr. Talon finally reaches us.

"What's going on here?" he asks in a voice that seems a little too soft to me. He saw the whole thing! He saw his daughter come within a whisker of being struck by this individual. Surely he should be more fired-up!

"And who are you?"

"I'm this little girl's father. If she has done you any harm, sir, then she will apologize."

"So you're her old man, are you? Well then, you can give her a good hiding right here in front of us. That'll teach her not to get in the way of merchants doing an honest trade."

"My name is Lucien Talon, at your service, sir. I will not hit my child, but I will be sure to give her a stern talking to so that she…"

"A 'stern talking to'? Are you kidding, Talon? And look at me when I'm talking to you. I am Pierre Duhaut. And this is my brother, Dominique Duhaut. And our partner, Jean L'Archevêque. We're no peasants like you! We're merchants with money and power. So now that you know who you're dealing with, you're going to do as I say. You're going to give her a good slap right—"

"No, I don't think so, Mr. Duhaut."

We turn around as one and see a man we hadn't noticed walk up to us. I have already seen him before. Crevel de Moranget is his name. He is Mr. De La Salle's nephew, a member of the navy. He wears his sword by his side and a pistol on his belt. He walks with a swagger and isn't always very polite to those around him, but right now I'm glad to see him.

"I don't think that Mr. Talon is going to beat the child."

"Mr. Moranget, this is none of your—"

"And why not, Mr. Duhaut?" the soldier interrupts, going face to face with him, which gives me the chance to see that he's taller by at least half a head. "As nephew to the leader of our expedition, it is my responsibility to maintain order aboard *L'Aimable*. It seems apparent to me that at this very moment, order has been a touch disrupted by all your shouting and waving."

"Come with me!" Marie-Élisabeth's father tells us.

To avoid us witnessing a quarrel that might well get out of hand, Mr. Talon gathers me, his daughter, Pierre, and Jean-Baptiste around him. He ushers us towards the opposite railing. As we walk, I look back to see what's happening between the two men.

"Very well," Pierre Duhaut grumbles at last. He makes the concession through gritted teeth, keeping his eyes locked on Moranget's. "Since you are the representative of order, sir, I cannot help but comply."

"A wise decision."

"But we'll meet again."

"No doubt, sir. We will be together for years to come."

"They're leaving, Mr. Talon," I murmur as we reach a very jittery Isabelle Talon on the other side of the boat. "There won't be a fight."

"That's something at least."

"We can thank Mr. Moranget for that," I add gratefully.

"Yes. Every pig has to work to keep this ship clean."

5

SPEAKING OF MR. DE LA SALLE

"What a wind!" I say to Marie-Élisabeth.

"Tell me about it!" replies Mr. Henri Joutel, Mr. De La Salle's lieutenant. "We are sailing large. In other words, the breeze is coming at an angle from behind us and seems slower due to the ship's speed. You'll see if we have to sail against a headwind or lie to in a storm."

Headwind? Lie to? It sounds like I still have plenty to learn. Not just about the wind, but about how sailors talk!

I liked the officer as soon as I saw him. He's a nice man, who's also fair and to the point, if you ask me.

"Excited by the voyage, big man?"

He just called me "big man"!

"Very, sir."

"That your little sister?"

Little? That's the very first time anyone has thought Marie-Élisabeth was younger than me.

"No, sir. She's my girl... my friend. Her name's Marie-Élisabeth Talon."

"My humble respects, miss," Mr. Joutel says to her, bowing his head.

"Sir," she whispers simply, repeating her mom's awkward curtsey.

The gentleman purses his lips and it seems to me that he's trying hard not to look amused. Henri Joutel must be older than twenty-five, but younger than thirty, I'd say. He's wearing a long, stylish pelt coat that shields him from the wind. His hat is even broader and has more feathers than Mr. De La Salle's. It adds a touch of class that only reinforces his authority. He smiles often, to everyone and anyone. He smiles no matter if you're an officer of the navy—or the son of a beggar woman like me.

Which is why he's often surrounded by sailors who enjoy making conversation with him.

"Were you with him, sir, when he discovered the Mississippi?" someone asks him. He's so short and stout he looks like a barrel.

"Mr. De La Salle, you mean?" says Henri Joutel, answering a question with a question. "No, I did not accompany him, but I have spoken with those who were there so often that I could tell you every last detail."

"Didn't he think that the river led on to India and China?"

"That's right! Only once he followed the Mississippi down to its mouth, Mr. De La Salle realized that the river flowed into Spanish waters: the Caribbean Sea. A discovery not to be sniffed at, let's be honest. That's something I bet even the Spanish didn't know. It was a huge victory for Mr. De La Salle and for our king to take possession of the whole territory on the kingdom's behalf. Louisiana will be French, not Spanish!"

A sickly-looking man, who fiddles nervously with his belt, risks a remark without daring to look Joutel in the eye.

"With all due respect, sir, I heard it said that many poked fun at Mr. De La Salle when he returned to his estate in Canada."

"And you are right," Joutel replies without a moment's hesitation, as though expecting the remark. "Derisively—and out of jealousy—a few comedians had great fun calling members of the Louisiana expedition the 'Chinese.' And today some still find it amusing to call De La Salle's estate on Saint-Sulpice, near Montréal, 'La Chine.'"

"Jealous, the lot of them!" says the sickly man. "Especially since Mr. De La Salle has the ear of the king."

"Well said, young man. His Majesty has granted titles and funds to our leader so that he might establish a colony near land claimed by our Spanish enemies. Proof indeed of the significance of his discovery."

"So that's why there was so much mystery surrounding our departure!" guffaws the sailor that looks like a barrel. "That's why we were told so often and so clearly not to say where we were off to. We're going to meet the source of the Mississippi and travel down the river to its mouth in Louisiana."

"No, my friends," says Joutel, to everyone's surprise. "We're not going upriver from the Mississippi, but directly to its mouth—via the Caribbean Sea!"

6

THE CEREMONY
UNDER THREAT

Half hidden by the huge canoe in the middle of the deck, three sailors pass by Marie-Élisabeth, Pierre, and me with a laugh. One of them covers his mouth to stifle his guffaws. Six more of their friends help them fill barrels with sea water.

"Sshh! Be quiet," one of them says, but is himself unable to suppress a chuckle.

"What are you doing?" asks Marie-Élisabeth.

"Drat! Kids!"

"I'm not a kid," I reply, putting a little more into it than I need to.

Because I'm not really angry. I'm used to it by now.

"You need to keep a secret! Can you do that?"

"Oh yes! Oh yes!" exclaims Pierre Talon.

He really is a kid.

"Come on, you're not going to tell them, are you?" one of the sailors protests.

"They're too young. We won't baptize them."

"Yes, we will!" vows a third. "Otherwise parents won't pay us for their kids. But we'll go easy on them. Just a few drops."

"There are already lots of people crossing the line for the first time... ha! ha!"

He finds the whole thing so funny that he can't go on. It's clear to look at Marie-Élisabeth, Pierre, and me that we don't have a clue what they're on about. So a sailor puts an arm around us and takes us to one side as he sees three passengers crossing the deck.

"You promise not to say a thing?" he asks us.

"I promise," I reply confidently, both to convince him and to show him that I'm the eldest, the leader of the trio.

"The ships will soon be crossing the line. And we—"

"The line?"

"The equator. The Earth's centre. Well, listen, so it's not really the line. We won't be that far south, but... ha! ha! ha! We've just come up with our own version of the old custom for the Tropic of Cancer. It's too funny! You won't want to miss a ceremony like this."

"And what exactly is the ceremony?"

"Tradition has it that each time a ship crosses the line, anyone who's already crossed it must 'baptize' those crossing it for the first time. They pour a little water over them, more if they kick up a fuss. Anyone who pays off the old hands is treated with more consideration and we sprinkle them—ha! ha!—a little less! The newly baptized must swear an oath never to let another soul cross the Equator—or in our case, the Tropic of Cancer—without being treated to the same rite of passage. Anyone who refuses to take part in the ceremony, well, let's just say we'll give them a good... ha! ha! ha!"

"Stop! Stop!"

Surprised, we turn around. I notice that the other sailors gathered around the barrels of water also stop what they're doing. They look puzzled. Two non-commissioned officers are approaching with an infantry lieutenant who is normally aboard *Le Joly*, but who came onto our ship this morning for something to do with supplies.

"What's going on here?" asks the sailor who had been explaining the baptism ceremony to us.

"What's going on is that the ceremony has been cancelled," the lieutenant replies.

"What?" The cry of surprise goes up as one from basically all the crew within earshot.

"But why?" one of them wonders.

"Mr. De La Salle says it is childish," replies an officer. "Passengers should not be subjected to a custom that serves only to take money from them. Especially since we are not crossing the Equator."

"But it's such fun!" another of the sailors protests.

"I am sorry, my friends," the lieutenant says, visibly disappointed. "We tried to explain your point of view to Mr. De La Salle, but there's nothing we can do."

"You can see he's no seafarer," a sailor grumbles, running an irritated hand across his bald head. "A true sailor wouldn't dare put an end to a tradition that dates back to... to..."

He motions with his hands to show that it's been going on too long for anyone to remember when exactly it started. What he doesn't mention is that the initiative to change the very same tradition for crossing the Tropic of Cancer was dreamt up by him and his friends.

"I'm very sorry, men," the lieutenant says again. "Please conduct yourselves according to the orders that come down from the leader. And those orders are to cancel all preparations for the ceremony."

The sailors had been having such a great time and now when the non-commissioned officers and the lieutenant leave they fly into a rage.

"No way! We can't let the passengers cross the line without getting baptized."

"We have no choice. Didn't you hear?"

"We swore at our own baptism not to let—"

"That was for the Equator. Not the Tropic of Cancer."

"That makes no difference! The tradition…"

"A plague on these dandies, on the minions of the court who rub shoulders with nobility and the king!"

"What an ass De La Salle is!"

"The Chinaman, you mean?"

As Marie-Élisabeth, Pierre Talon, and I walk away from the raging men, it saddens me to hear them speak ill of our expedition's leader.

Little do I know that, as the days and months go by, I'll hear worse, much worse, about him.

7

THE HAPPIEST
TWO SETTLERS

One night I am woken up by the first cries of a newborn baby. I am lying against a pile of sails propped up by what's known as the ship's web frame. In the nook beside me, half lit by oil lamps held by two women, I can see the mother's back. It's dark, but more light is out of the question because of the risk of fire. Fire is what all sailors are most afraid of. One of the two shipmasters in charge of *L'Aimable* has told us to be careful I don't know how many times.

But it was unthinkable for Mrs. Talon to give birth out on deck in plain view. And so the women are huddled around her in this corner of the hold. The ship's surgeon is also hovering in the background in case he might have to slice her open with a barber's razor. Sometimes the babies refuse to come out, that's what the midwives say. With the fate that lies in store for them if ever their mothers were to be widowed, I must say I can't blame them.

"It's just a boy, Stache!" Marie-Élisabeth says, leaving the group of women to come over to me.

She shrugs and rolls her eyes. Her father has just been given the news and is being patted on the back. He raises his fist in victory.

"So? Won't a little brother be great?"

"Ugh!" she pouts, dropping down to sit beside me. "I already have three brothers. And you're my boyfriend. That's plenty of boys around me as it is."

Her boy...? She said *I* was her boy...friend?

"And I have only one sister. Another girl would have been nice to help me give Mom a hand."

Her boyfriend? Her boyfriend?

"Just imagine, father to a son who's going to be given a seigneury," three or four passengers are saying, spreading the news around Mr. Talon.

I'm Marie-Élisabeth's boyfriend! I'm the happiest settler in the world. Happier even than Mr. Talon. Who's still celebrating with his friends.

A woman walks past the group, muttering to herself. I know her. She's the wife of Mr. Barbier, the pilot of *L'Aimable*.

"We'll see," she says. "Royal privilege was for the first child born in the colony. We're still on our way there. We're not in Louisiana yet."

"She's just jealous," a man mumbles once she has gone.

"Is it our fault if the ships have been delayed?" a second man pipes up.

"Or if God decided the babe be born two weeks ahead of time?" chips in a third.

Mr. Talon is too happy that Providence has given him a fourth son for the words of a jealous woman to dampen his excitement. He continues to celebrate.

"And Mr. De La Salle has agreed to be the godfather," he tells the crowd. "We will call him Robert."

Mr. Talon happens to catch my eye. He raises his fist in victory. I do the same.

We're the happiest two settlers in the world.

8

RAISED VOICES

All is not well on board. Conditions are rough and the sailors are worried that what's known as a "hurricane" in these parts might be on its way. We don't know the like of such storms in Europe.

"The winds can lift a ship and flip it right over, drowning everyone on board."

The sailors pray, the passengers and soldiers vomit, and the pigs have a great time of things.

Worse still, fifty or so people are suffering from all kinds of illnesses. They include not only the surgeons, but Mr. De La Salle himself.

"We're running out of fresh water," Lucien Talon tells his wife and my mom. "The sailors say we'll have to land on the island of Saint-Domingue soon. We've been at sea for close to sixty days. It's time we arrived."

"This morning I overheard two Recollects say that Captain Beaujeu passed by Port-de-Paix overnight. They say we're much further on," replies Isabelle Talon, her newborn on her breast.

"We've already passed Saint-Domingue?"

"Not the island, just Port-de-Paix. We're going to moor at Petit-Goâve, or so they say."

"Without Mr. De La Salle's go-ahead?"

"That's what the Recollects were saying."

"But why would Captain Beaujeu have done such a thing?" asks Mom.

Isabelle Talon shrugs, causing the baby to lose her nipple for a moment.

"Things are tense between both men," her husband replies, shaking his head. "I think they're both jealous of each other."

"Let's hope things get back to normal soon," Mom sighs, "before it disrupts our colony."

Especially since I myself have seen our leader rebuked more than a few times. I hope things don't get any worse.

But my mom doesn't look fearful or worried.

Ever since we left La Rochelle, she's been happy. At least, she's been much calmer than back when we were begging on the street. She finds plenty to keep her busy with the Talons, which helps her forget about my dad and little brother. And even though the food could be better, we can eat every day without having to demean ourselves. Without having to endure the scorn on the faces of passersby or the priest's lecherous advances.

She extends an arm to me and holds me tight. It's been happening more and more since Armand died. I can't stand it: it feels like she's still treating me like a child. And Marie-Élisabeth might think I'm the one asking to be hugged like a big baby.

But I know Mom is doing it to replace the hugs she will no longer get from my younger brother. And perhaps also to enjoy these moments of affection we share together in case I might die, too.

So I might not like it, but I let her act like my mom. I owe her that.

Mom and I are very excited. For the first time in our lives we see forests of strange trees, plants with huge leaves, remarkable exotic fruit, colourful birds that make unusual sounds, monkeys, crocodiles, and other animals I don't know the first thing about.

We marvel at everything each time we get the chance to go ashore. And even from the deck of *L'Aimable*, we can wonder at the explosion of flora and fauna that is completely foreign to us. The Talons might already be familiar with North America, but they're just as excited as we are.

But not today. Today, no one is admiring anything at all.

We've been docked at the port of Petit-Goâve for a week now and the birds' cheeping is suddenly drowned out by raised voices. Even from our ship, *L'Aimable*, we can hear Mr. De La Salle laying into Captain Beaujeu on *Le Joly*. The captain remains impassive, claiming not to take offence, although I'm sure that inside he must be furious with our expedition leader.

"I wonder if docking in Petit-Goâve rather than Port-de-Paix is really so detrimental to our undertaking," a Recollect wonders out loud, leaning against the gunwale.

I'm close by him, sitting on the rat line, holding on to the shrouds of the main mast—the webbed rigging that links the top of the masts to the railing.

"It's more about obeying a superior's orders," replies Henri

Joutel, not sounding as though he cares one way or another.

Captain Beaujeu says that, as the man in charge of the vessel, it is up to him to determine the best places to dock. Mr. De La Salle counters that he is responsible for everything. Who's right and who's wrong? I don't like seeing the men leading our expedition arguing, especially not in public. No good can come of it.

"Either way, Captain Beaujeu's initiative has led to the *Saint-François* losing its way north of Saint-Domingue," remarks a second priest just below me. "We can only hope we do not have to wait too long before the ketch finds us here."

I glance back down at the deck and see Marie-Élisabeth, not far from the forecastle. She's holding Madeleine's hand. I presume they're coming back from the head, the place at the front of the boat where we go to the bathroom. The girls weave their way through the interlaced rigging that runs down from the top of the masts to the pin rails on the upper deck and the railing.

Standing against the rigging, a huge hulk of a man with a thick bronze-coloured beard, long sunburned hair, and irises as grey as a stormy sea watches them pass by, not letting them out of his sight. He is clutching a knife, its blade polished like new, with a bone handle that is cracked in the centre. He's using it to carve a piece of wood.

I know that his name is Hiens. When I was on the wharf in Petit-Goâve helping the sailors move barrels of food, I heard him telling the big man who took on volunteers who he was. He was recruited, along with a few others of his build, to replace some of our own men who deserted as soon as we reached land.

Hiens is from Germany, which explains his thick accent. When they asked him what he did for a living, he replied, "I kill. I was a freebooter on the boat that left me here."

His answer drew a laugh from Mr. De La Salle. He said he liked men like Hiens: they didn't desert at the first sniff of danger.

Despite the—debatable—qualities a freebooter could bring to an expedition like ours, I don't like Hiens very much. I don't like the way he ogles Marie-Élisabeth and Madeleine. I don't like the gap-toothed smiles he gives them.

And I especially don't like the hand he tries to slip beneath their skirts when the two little Talon girls walk past.

9

GREY SPLOTCHES

On this early October morning, still at the wharf in Petit-Goâve, terrible news is spreading: the *Saint-François* has been taken by a Spanish patrol. Mr. De La Salle and Captain Beaujeu are quickly at each other's throats again. Mr. De La Salle is holding the captain responsible for the loss since he didn't follow orders. The captain of *Le Joly* doesn't have much of a defence: neither storms nor a difficult approach prevented him docking in Port-de-Paix. Just pride.

"Our tools, equipment, nails... everything we needed to build our shelters," despairs Mr. Talon with a shake of the head. "All because the ketch couldn't keep up with the others. How stupid these officers and noblemen can be!"

"I've already seen you build a lean-to with nothing but branches and a few loose ends of rope," his wife consoles him. "You're the finest carpenter I know."

"Mr. De La Salle looked high and low for men like you for a reason, Lucien," says my mom. "He knows what you can do with the means at your disposal. It's men like you that our expedition depends on, not our leaders."

"But they'll get all the glory once the colony is up and running," laughs Lucien Talon, with a hint of bitterness in his voice.

I laugh with the three adults while Pierre and Jean-Baptiste, too young to understand the conversation's nuances, make do with staring at us. Robert the newborn, lying in a blanket at his mother's side, wakes and demands to be fed. As she puts him to her breast, Mrs. Talon asks Ludovic to go help Madeleine who has caught her foot in a pile of ropes she was trying to climb.

"And Marie-Élisabeth?" she asks, leaning against the wooden frame behind her. "She's taking her time coming back from the head. I bet some of the sailors have caught a fish or two and she's bombarding them with her usual questions. Lucien, can you go get her before one of the fishermen throws her overboard?"

"It's fine, Mr. Talon," I say. "I'll go."

And I leap up before he has a chance to protest.

"Of course he will. He *loves* her!" Pierre Talon shouts behind me.

I can hear Mrs. Talon giggle as I reach the ladder up to the deck. She whispers to my mother, but loudly enough for me to hear.

"It's so nice to see. Perhaps they'll be the first to wed in the colony."

Mom's laughter is lost at my feet as I reach the top of the hatch.

"Have you seen Marie-Élisabeth?"

"Your girlfriend?" the two sailors at the bow reply. "We did, not long ago. But she's not here now."

"Have you seen Marie-Élisabeth?"

"The little Talon girl?" asks the Recollect without looking up from the full basket of fish being hauled aboard. "No. Or rather, yes! A good quarter of an hour ago."

"Have you seen Marie-Élisabeth?"

"Who? Your mom?" grumbles the quartermaster who has just been given his daily brandy ration and doesn't appreciate being interrupted.

"No, my friend Marie-Élisabeth."

"Oh, her! I just saw her with Hiens. She was helping him carry his clothes."

"What do you mean his clothes?"

"I mean his clothes! He had done his washing and she was giving him a hand bringing his stuff back to his hammock."

A very bad feeling suddenly comes over me. Marie-Élisabeth might have wanted to help Hiens, but I'm worried about his real intentions.

"Where is Hiens's hammock?"

"Whose hammock...? Oh, right! Beneath the fo'c'sle with the rest of the topmen. Now will you leave me alone?"

I don't even thank him and race off to the front of the ship. Running across a deck strewn with rigging and ropes of all kinds—halyards, stays, and shrouds—is no mean feat.

"*Holà*, kid! Don't run like that," a sailor scolds me. "You're gonna break a leg against a pin rail."

"Or hurt an honest cook," the ship's cook chimes in, more amused than angry.

It feels like it takes me an eternity to reach the dark lair where sailors on the nightshift sleep. As I walk into the tiny room, the light goes out as though I'd blown on a candle. It takes a second or two for my eyes to adjust from bright sunlight to a dark room.

"Marie-Élisabeth?"

There's a thump against my shoulder and a man groans. A sailor has just tossed in his bed, a single sheet nailed to the wall. He didn't hit me on purpose; I just didn't notice I was right beside him.

I lower my voice and call out again.

"Marie-Élisabeth? Are you there?"

I can see better now. Four hammocks are hanging from the long bulkhead where the men are asleep. I hear snoring, groans, and snorting, but no answer.

"Marie-Élisabeth?"

"Back there," grumbles a gruff, sleep-filled voice.

Back there is in total darkness. If my friend is here and I can't see her, it stands to reason that she is—

"*Geh weg!*"

I recognize the man who bumps into me as he strides to the door. It's Hiens. I don't know what that meant in German, but it sure doesn't sound friendly.

"Marie-Élisabeth?"

"They said 'Back there,' pighead!" the freebooter shouts in his terrible accent before disappearing into the light outside.

I walk toward the dark corner the brute has just bounded out of. I get down on all fours to slip beneath two hammocks that are fixed to the ceiling and sagging with so much weight.

When I glimpse my friend right in the corner, I'm just about to walk into her. She has her back to the wall, her knees tucked below her chin, her arms wrapped around her legs, her skirt tight against the floor beneath her feet.

"Marie-Élisabeth? Why didn't you answer?"

"Go away, Stache!"

I'm more surprised than upset by her tone. She must be afraid of Hiens.

"He's gone, the big oaf. Come on."

"Let me be!"

"Come on!" I say again. "Your parents sent me to look for you. They were worried."

Instead of replying or getting up, she bursts into tears.

"Marie-Élisabeth, but what's—"

"She shouldn't have bitten him."

I jump. The voice came from above my head. It's one of the sailors in his hammock. All I can see is the silhouette of his thick head of hair.

"Bitten him?" I ask in surprise. "He must have deserved it."

"And a little bit more, yes. But he flew into a rage. He lost his temper with the girl. Otherwise he'd have paid attention."

"Attention to what?"

I turn back to Marie-Élisabeth.

"What did he do to you?"

"Nothing! Nothing!"

My friend shoves me away as she gets back to her feet. I lose my balance and fall.

"She shouldn't have done that," the voice above me continues. "It got him all worked up."

"If you saw everything, then why didn't you help her? She's just a little girl up against a brute like that!"

"Ain't none of our business, kid, what goes on in the bunks in the dark. You'll learn that for yourself. Ain't none of our business."

I don't really understand what the sailor is getting at, but my time's up. Marie-Élisabeth is heading for the door. I follow.

As she ducks into the passageway leading outside, I notice that her skirt is torn. There's blood on her leg, mixed in with grey splotches.

"Marie-Élisabeth! What did he do to you?"

She whirls around so quickly that I take a step back. The blue of her eyes is now tinged with purple, tiny little red veins staining the white eyeballs. They are full of anger and disgust. Suffering, too! I don't know how to react to such mixed emotions. One thing is for sure: I won't be asking any more questions.

My friend's mouth opens on either side of two rows of clenched teeth. A little foam gathers at its corner.

"Shut up, Stache," she hisses. "You'll never—do you hear me? never!—tell a soul where you found me, how you found me, who you found me with! Is that clear?"

I'm rooted to the spot. It's not the Marie-Élisabeth I know. At least not the little ten-year-old girl who, mature as she might be, is still a little ten-year-old. But she looks like her own mother all of a sudden. An angry version of her own mother.

"Is that clear?"

"I... Yes, Marie-Élisabeth. Don't wo—"

"You can tell them I fell up at the head. That's all. That's where I tore my dress."

"O… OK."

And as we bring back a bucket of sea water so that she can wash her legs, I realize that from this day forward Marie-Élisabeth will never ever be a little girl again.

10

SAILING LESSON

The ships are back at sea, sailing toward the mouth of the Mississippi.

"West by northwest!"

I love hearing the pilot of *L'Aimable*, Mr. Barbier, shout instructions like this to his helmsman. The helmsman tells me all about the manoeuvres he has to make.

"You see? I push the helm until the needle points in the right direction. Then I keep her steady to stay on course. Give me a hand, would you? You stand here. Keep the tiller nice and steady. You can really feel the waves in your shoulders, can't you? The currents are against us. They're taking us east to Florida. But we've been well warned. That's why we're headed northwest. That way if we drift, we'll loop back to where we're headed. We're making up for it, see?"

"I see," I say, pouting to show that I know all about it. "But there's no land in sight. How do you know where we are?"

"The pilot has instruments for that. Using the angle of the stars in the sky or the height of the midday sun, he can easily work out the ship's latitude. It's the longitude that's hard."

"You're like two old women, you two," Barbier grumbles alongside us, trying to concentrate on his maps. "Stop jabbering away, would you?"

"What's longitude?" I ask the helmsman, ignoring Barbier's grumbling.

"The distance travelled from east to west," he replies, glancing at the compass. "We have to estimate it. In other words, we more or less know where we are. Mr. De La Salle and the pilot of *Le Joly* think we're too close to Apalachee Bay at the minute. So we're making up for it by heading much further west."

"More or less."

"More or less, yes."

"And when will we arrive, do you think? In a day? A week? A month?"

"More or less, yes," he says again and bursts out laughing. He doesn't have a clue, I decide.

The wind blows my long hair across my face. I brush it away, breathing in a good lungful of fresh sea air. My lips taste of salt and my skin is more tanned than it has ever been before.

I like sailing.

I would be happier still if Marie-Élisabeth hadn't begun to keep her distance from me. It hurts. It's like she's angry at me for knowing the terrible secret we share. As though what happened to her is partly my fault. But I'd cut both my arms off for the sadness to leave her heart and for her to become the Marie-Élisabeth of before.

Her parents have also noticed her change in attitude, her constant bouts of melancholy, her sullenness. But they put it down to all the time at sea. Too long, they say.

More than once I've caught Marie-Élisabeth scrubbing her legs, right where I saw the red and grey stains running down them. Right where the stains seeped through.

"You're going to ruin your skin with all that salt water," Barbier's wife has told her more than once.

Marie-Élisabeth only muttered a reply. It didn't sound very nice to me. I pretended not to have heard a thing.

PART III

America

II

NAKED LIKE ANIMALS

"Land!"

The shout surprises no one. For two days, the men in charge have suspected we've been nearing land: because of the change in currents, the new colour of the water, the birds circling above us—birds that haven't always been the same as the ones we saw out at sea—and even because of the type of silt and coral the lead sounding lines have been bringing back up with them.

"Do you think it's the Bay of the Holy Spirit, sir?" Henri Joutel asks our expedition leader. "The mouth of the Mississippi?"

"The sand bars are certainly similar," De La Salle replies. "But we won't really know until we get out and do some exploring."

Today I'm on *La Belle* with a few ship's boys who are barely two years older than me. It's our job to carry letters between the ships' captains. I think they're getting ready for an important meeting of Mr. De La Salle's officers and first mates tonight. They know we're close to our goal.

For hours now we've been sailing with just one sail—and a small one at that!—because the sounders up front want .

to make sure the water is deep enough that we don't risk running aground.

The next day, we're treated to quite the show.

When a few weeks ago I caught sight of the flora and fauna of the Americas, the wonderment and curiosity I felt was nothing compared to how I feel now. For the very first time, I can see what the seasoned travellers have been talking about for months: Savages!

They approached us this morning when our people went on a reconnaissance mission with the rowboats. Some agreed to come up onto the ships in return for the tiny bells, knives, and mirrors we gave them as presents. I'm absolutely fascinated.

Since they live as naked as the animals of the forest, I can describe their anatomy—apart from their private parts, which they keep hidden behind a loincloth wrapped around their waists. They are quite tall and muscular. Their faces are handsome, but they make themselves uglier by painting shapes and strange symbols on their skin. Their hair, which they keep very long behind their backs, has feathers on top and they—

"They are nothing but animals," says Pierre Duhaut, the lout who once tried to hit Marie-Élisabeth because he had walked into her.

"The Recollects say they have souls to be converted, but I scarcely know of a Christian Savage," his brother Dominique adds.

"There's Nika," says Jean L'Archevêque, the third member of the inseparable trio.

Nika. I had forgotten all about him. It's true that he dresses like a European. He works with Mr. De La Salle's servants. I think he has been with our leader ever since he discovered the Mississippi three or four years ago. Perhaps longer. He's from the Shawnee tribe.

"Those ones are more primitive than Nika," says Dominique Duhaut. "They don't understand Nika or any of the other tongues of the Mississippi that De La Salle has tried to use on them."

I take two steps forward. I want to tell the men that, if you ask me, it's not because the nations speak different dialects that one is superior to the other, but I catch Pierre Duhaut's eye. I wonder if he remembers who I am. If he remembers it was me who threw a pulley at his shoulder.

I decide to keep a low profile instead and go back to the ship's boys.

It's safer that way.

12

ON DRY LAND

"Oh, Lord Jesus! Lord Jesus! Promise me you'll be careful."

"Of course I will, Mom!"

My mom holds me tight against her. When I manage to free myself from her hug, Mr. Talon gives me a wink.

"It's not the first trip ashore, Delphine," he says. "We know the Indians are peaceful and willing to help us. What's more, Eustache has sworn to stay right by my side. Isn't that right, lad?"

"You be careful, too," Isabelle Talon retorts, pretending to glare at her husband.

"I want to go, too, Dad," Pierre Talon shouts, even though he's only eight. "I'm not a baby anymore."

"Sorry, Pierre," his father replies. "Mr. De La Salle says boys must be at least twelve to go ashore with the group. Eustache can leave the ship, but you can't."

"What about me? What about me?" pleads Jean-Baptiste, clinging to his mother's skirt.

I turn toward Marie-Élisabeth, but she looks away. She pretends to be caught up in darning a piece of clothing belonging to one of her brothers. I would have appreciated a goodbye smile. Despite her change in attitude and her new-found indifference to me, I still love her just as much. I wish I didn't know what happened to her. That way, there wouldn't be this dark secret between us, a secret that doesn't bring us closer, but instead drives us apart.

Perhaps time will help. Perhaps one day she'll go back to being the kind Marie-Élisabeth of old, once the sorrow Hiens the freebooter left inside her has been diluted.

Perhaps.

I follow Mr. Talon. After one last kiss for his wife, he climbs the ladder through the main hatchway and up onto the deck. We go back to the group of one hundred and twenty volunteers who are taking their places in the rowboats.

"Look, Eustache! Look!"

Just like me, Mr. Talon has just seen a buffalo for the first time. Just like me, he's very excited.

The animals are a little like cows covered in sheep's wool. They are absolutely enormous, their heads disproportionately big compared to the rest of their bodies. Their eyes on either side of the head are so far away from each other that they can see as much behind them as ahead of them. That's what the Natives say, at least.

Some of us have been appointed hunters for the group. They fire four times and as many animals fall to the ground—delicious! After weeks of dry biscuits, salted fish, and stagnant water, it feels good to eat fresh meat and drink our fill.

"Brr! And they said it was going to be warm here," Mr. Talon mutters through chattering teeth. "It feels like I'm back in Canada."

"Yep! But our fine young dandies don't seem too concerned by our shivering," moans Oris, a sailor from *L'Aimable*. His mouth is half full as he motions toward De La Salle, Joutel, Father Cavelier, and Moranget with his knife.

"Now, now, don't be unfair," Lucien Talon replies. "They're cold, too."

"But they have nice big coats and keep close to the fire." He's not wrong.

But with the hide of a hare that Marie-Élisabeth's dad killed earlier over my shoulders, I don't feel too bad.

"The man is a fool! He's incapable of accepting that we know more than him, that we are better than him—and senior to him!"

The raised voice belongs to Mr. De La Salle. It's not hard to work out that he means Captain Beaujeu. Both men have been at loggerheads since we left La Rochelle. Instead of bringing them together, the dangers we have faced along the way, the storms at sea, the loss of the *Saint-François*, the ups and downs of the voyage, seem only to have deepened their differences. Worse still, factions seem to be forming: those who agree with one, and those who are behind the other.

"We're going to end up with two different factions, if we don't watch out," sighs Mr. Talon, who's thinking just like me. "That doesn't augur well for the colony. We'll end up divided. Or worse, at odds with each other."

"We've found a frozen lake less than a league away," Desfloges suddenly announces, coming over to sit with the ten or so people who make up our little team. "And a freshwater river. Maybe it's the Mississippi everyone's so keen to find."

A shrug or two show the sailor that his news is of little interest to us. So Desfloges lowers his voice and adds mysteriously:

"We also found a dead Indian."

Heads turn to face him. His half smile shows that he's happy to have piqued our interest.

"Throat slit from ear to ear," he adds.

"Were they fighting among themselves?" a sailor asks.

"His tattoos were the same as the other Savages' who come to see us from time to time," Desfloges replies. "He wasn't from an enemy tribe."

"It's Indian custom to scalp their enemies," adds Oris. "Was he scalped?"

"No," says Desfloges. "And the body we found had his hands tied behind his back with a hemp rope."

"Hemp?" Oris asks, surprised. "But the Indians don't have..."

"It was one of ours that killed him."

13

THE NATIVES ATTACK

In February 1685, our team is still ashore. Out on the water, the pilots aboard *L'Aimable* and *La Belle* are sounding the river to find the best channel. They want to pass the ships through because we think we're on one of the shores of the Mississippi Delta. At least, that's what Mr. De La Salle says. But he's not quite sure. It's the right latitude. But this darned latitude, which we can only more or less work out, is causing the problem.

Sometimes, weather permitting, we can make out the people watching us from the ships in the distance. Sometimes I wave at Mom, and at Marie-Élisabeth...

It's strange to be so near and yet so far.

"Mr. Joutel, can you ask eight volunteers to cut down that big tree over there, near the bend in the river? It would make an excellent canoe."

"Certainly, sir."

Lucien Talon and I happen to be right beside them, adding wood to the fire of the men who lead us.

"You're a carpenter, aren't you?" Henri Joutel asks Marie-Élisabeth's father.

"I am indeed, sir."

"So there's a job for you."

And so I find myself wading upriver with Lucien Talon, the marquis de La Sablonnière, Desfloges, Oris, and the three inseparable beasts: the Duhaut brothers and Jean L'Archevêque. At first I was still worried about how the elder Duhaut brother might react to me being there, but I quickly discover that he is completely indifferent to me. He's either forgotten, or he's not one to hold a grudge.

Or else he thinks I'm so insignificant that I was no worse than a mosquito, irritating him for a second or two.

We don't see the Natives until they're already upon us. There are twenty or so painted warriors, brandishing leather shields, spears, flint knives, and tomahawks (a weapon that is basically just a rock on the end of a stick).

Six of our own are surrounded. The Duhaut brothers were off by themselves—one to pee in the bushes, the other chasing a partridge—and manage to get away. They'll alert the others.

We're not armed, apart for the marquis de La Sablonnière who has a sword. But by the time he manages to draw it, two sharp points are already pressed against his chest, ready to bore into him at the first sign of resistance.

With his axe, Oris manages to drive back the first attacker to rush at him. This earns him a club to the head and he collapses, unconscious in the mud.

Lucien Talon and I, standing side by side, are immediately facing two tomahawks and a long flint knife. We show no sign of rebelliousness or a desire to flee.

I'm too stunned to really grasp what's going on. And strangely enough what makes me saddest of all is less my fate than the needless brutality the two Natives show toward Lucien Talon. They shove him in the back with their weapons, believing no doubt that I'm just a child. One of them hauls me along by the arm, without really hurting me.

Oris is still unconscious and is dragged away by the feet. His head bumps against rocks and roots along the way. Desfloges is in tears, imploring his torturers—unmoved, they seem only to treat him more roughly than ever—while Jean L'Archevêque swears at them with oaths that almost leave me blushing. Only the marquis de La Sablonnière surprises his captors by walking more quickly than them, with the arched back of a *hidalgo*, impervious to their slaps and the scratches their spears leave behind.

"Are you OK, Eustache?"

"I'm OK, Mr. Talon."

We reach the top of a knoll that's bare of vegetation. I almost shout out with surprise. It's the first time I've seen a Native village.

Fifty or so dome-shaped huts are scattered around. They are made from bulrushes and dried animal hides draped over curved poles. Hundreds of naked Natives, all brightly painted and wearing feathers or shells, watch us arrive in silence. I'm pleasantly surprised: the girls have their breasts, bellies, butts, and legs on display for all to see. I pretend not to notice.

Everyone is staring at us. There's no doubt it's the first time these villagers have ever set eyes on Europeans. Our features, our pale plain skin, the hair on the adults' faces, our clothes… Everything is new to them, too. And some look worried. Some Natives, it seems, are annoyed that we were brought here.

In a strange, guttural language…

"It sounds like a hen clucking after her young," Jean L'Archevêque mutters scornfully.

…in a strange language, as I was saying, a bent-over old man—who looks to me to be their chief—is hurling abuse at the man who led our captors here.

The two argue for a moment until the warrior gives in. He leaves us and strides over to a hut, venting his anger by pushing over a pot full of gruel that had been hanging from a wooden trammel over the fire. A woman scolds him and drags him inside.

It might have been funny in different circumstances. But nobody so much as cracks a smile. Least of all Oris. He has come to and is looking around groggily, an enormous bump on the side of his head.

The chief walks over and looks us up and down in silence, walking through the middle of our group. He finishes his inspection in front of me, shaking his head, as though saying to himself, "And they even kidnapped a child." It might have reassured me. But instead it annoys me, as usual.

Then again, maybe that's not quite what the old man is thinking.

He has a kindly face, not too quiet, rather conciliatory. He motions to the captors and for a moment I think it's to let us go and ask us to go back to where we came from. But that's not what happens.

"Hey! Easy does it, you Savages! Easy does it!"

Oris grumbles as he is shoved forward with a spear so that a Native who is wearing even more feathers and paint than the others can examine his bump.

"He must be the village medicine man. A sorcerer," Lucien Talon ventures.

Oris is brought over to this doctor of sorts and we are urged to gather again among the huts. Still with the help of their weapons, they make us sit around the fire. A dog's carcass is roasting over it and a clay cooking pot sits to one side. It's full of a thick-looking soup.

"It's called sagamité," Marie-Élisabeth's father tells me. "It's boiled corn and meat scraps."

"Is it good?"

"When you're really hungry, yes."

But Lucien Talon is laying it on too thick. When the women begin to dish it out in big banana leaves, I find it delicious.

"Don't eat it, kid," Desfloges tells me in a shaky voice. "They're out to avenge their compatriot, the one we found dead. They're poisoning us."

"What are you talking about?" De La Sablonnière retorts, bringing the sagamité to his lips. "If they want to kill us, they have plenty of spears."

His logic doesn't convince Desfloges, and Jean L'Archevêque laughs as he wolfs down a huge mouthful.

Our captors have been forbidden from approaching us, and for the rest of the evening the women lavish us with attention—they give us food and water, they run their hands through our hair, they even give long, lingering kisses to

Oris, who is back with us now, a leaf dressing covering his wound. For prisoners, we're being rather well looked after.

"They're afraid we'll retaliate," Lucien Talon whispers to me, as though afraid the Natives might understand. "Some of them saw the arquebuses in action when they came to visit us. They must have told the elders that, if they mistreat us, they will be massacred when Mr. De La Salle comes to demand we are set free."

"Do you think we will be held prisoner for long?" I ask, a little frightened all the same.

"I'm sure we'll be free again very, very soon."

14

THUNDER
IN THE BLUE SKY

They split us up. We each spend the night in a different hut. Maybe the Natives are frightened we'll work together to plan our escape. After all, it's easier to keep an eye on a single prisoner alone in his corner than six who might be up to something.

And so I end up with a family where I quickly become a game for the children. They are between two and six years old. The parents let them walk up to me, touch me, then jump all over me. I make them laugh, holding them upside down, rocking them back and forth, and pretending to be their horse.

In the morning, when a big group of men armed with arquebuses arrives in the village hot on the heels of Mr. De La Salle, I greet our liberators with a kid on my shoulders and two more clinging to my pants.

Our men—who seem mighty pleased to find us alive— look the part: gruff and aggressive. They are constantly blowing on the matchlock wicks of their muskets, coaxing them back to life. I'm pleased to see that the common enemy seems to have rallied everyone together.

The old man who had been rebuking our captors' leader the night before and who seems to be the village chief walks forward with a stoop to meet the leader of our expedition. He runs a bony hand across his own chest before doing the same to De La Salle. He repeats the strange gesture on his arm, then on De La Salle's.

"It's OK," De La Salle shouts to us, without taking his eyes off the chief. "It's a sign of peace. He's demonstrating his friendship. But don't let your guard down. Make sure there isn't a group of them waiting discreetly off to the side. They can be more cunning than foxes."

When the chief has finished his friendly ritual, he explains in his strange language things that even Mr. De La Salle doesn't seem to understand a word of—and this from a man who knows a great many nations along the Mississippi. The old man points to me and the other prisoners and for a moment I think it's to ask us to go back to our friends. But Mr. De La Salle interprets for us.

"The old rascal would like a gift or two in exchange for freeing our people."

"A gift or two? He must be joking!" grumbles his nephew Moranget, raising his arquebus. "I'll give them every shot from my musket. How about that?"

"Calm down," growls De La Salle. "I don't want to get on the wrong side of them. We have enough problems to resolve among us as it is, without adding to them."

Our leader leaves the old man and comes across to De La Sablonnière, who as a nobleman and infantry lieutenant, can speak for our group.

"Were you manhandled, marquis?" he asks him.

"No, sir," he replies right away, looking scornfully at Moranget. "These people were perfectly proper with us. They fed us and received us amiably."

De La Salle stares at the wound on Oris's head but doesn't say a word.

"Mr. Oris tried to kill a Savage with his axe, sir," De La Sablonnière explains. "The Indian was simply defending himself."

I suddenly realize that the children surrounding me have left and are now a few paces behind me. The kid who had been sitting on my shoulders is in his mom's arms. Parents are discreetly sending their little ones back to the huts. Here and there, I can see other couples doing the same. A clash is in the air.

De La Salle hesitates a while longer in front of Oris, then turns to speak to the village leader.

"Very well," he says. "We shall consider the incident closed if your chief—"

BOOOOOOM!

He is interrupted by a noise like thunder, loud and unexpected in equal measure. All the Natives throw themselves to the ground, shrieking in terror. The women beg for mercy, the children are in tears, the men are stunned and frightened.

It must be said that such a commotion in a clear blue sky is enough to surprise anyone unaccustomed to it.

Only we Europeans do not gaze heavenward. Instead, we look over to the bay at the foot of the slope. The trees and hills stand in our way, but our liberators seem to know what's going on.

"It's *L'Aimable*," Barbier whispers. "I'd recognize that cannon anywhere."

"It's the distress signal," says Henri Joutel. "It's on the sand bar."

"I knew it!" De La Salle says, trying to contain his rage. But he looks more worried than angry. "They must have run the ship aground."

"We don't have a minute to waste talking to these damned Savages, sir," splutters Moranget. "Let's put a few holes in a chest or two to free our men and let the soulless beasts consider the consequences of their actions."

De La Salle doesn't respond to his nephew directly. He turns back to the Indian chief to ask for our freedom. The man is already standing, too proud to let fear keep him on the ground. He motions that he will let the prisoners go without further ado.

"Very well," says De La Salle, lowering the barrel of Moranget's arquebus with his hand while he looks at the chief. "Mr. Joutel?"

"Sir?"

"Hand out a few trinkets to these braves so that they see there is more to be gained by working with us than against us."

"With pleasure, sir."

I can see the relief and satisfaction on Henri Joutel's face as he rummages around in a bag at his feet. The same can't be said for Moranget, a quarrelsome individual, who seems deeply disappointed by our leader's conciliatory attitude.

"But, Uncle," he says. "If we're so weak... I mean... generous with them, they'll attack again just to take advantage of our generosity when the time comes to negotiate our prisoners' release. If we kill a few of them now, they'll learn their lesson and leave us in peace."

Our leader turns to his nephew. I can't see his face from where I'm standing, but one thing is for sure: judging by Moranget's disappointed expression, De La Salle doesn't share his opinion.

"Better this than make enemies of them, Crevel, believe me. I saw them fight at the Mississippi. Their weapons might be less powerful than our own, Crevel, but when they fight... My God, when they fight..."

Moranget's face crumples and he gives in sullenly. When he at last points his musket back at the ground, I lose interest in him. Henri Joutel, showing off a broad grin amidst his bushy beard, hands out bracelets and bells to the Natives, who yelp with delight. My friends have already taken the path leading out of the village. I'm about to set off after them when I feel something grabbing at my pants.

I turn around and find myself face to face with one of the kids from the night before. He's come back out of the hut to find me.

I can't get rid of him until I've given him a big hug.

15

THE BIRTHDAY

"A cake?"

Mom is crying her heart out as she hands me a little golden ball wrapped in a handkerchief. We're sitting on the rocks down by the river, getting ready to set up a first camp on shore without really knowing if it will be permanent.

"For your birthday," she replies.

"My birth— It's my birthday?"

"You're thirteen. You turned thirteen yesterday or the day before, I'm not sure."

And she sobs even louder. Behind her, the sinister silhouette of *L'Aimable* lurches out on the water. Waves break against her yards, sending out creamy ripples of foam. The ship has run aground in the shallows, outside of the buoys that Barbier, the pilot, had nonetheless been careful to draw attention to.

Water flooded steerage, and the sailors were unable to salvage many supplies. But they rush to move our provisions onto land in case a storm topples or sinks the ship for good.

L'Aimable is now amiable in name only.

"Congratulations, big lad!" Lucien Talon says to me, with a pat on the back. "This time you really are a man."

"Oh! Not for another year," says Mom between sobs. "He's still so small. I mean… so young."

"In a little while," Isabelle Talon goes on, "it will be Marie-Élisabeth's birthday, too. She was born in March. Eleven, she'll be. Then Jean-Baptiste will be eight. Pierre, nine… Their birthdays are all about two weeks apart."

Again without any warning, Mom holds me tight, wetting my hair with her tears. She was so frightened when she heard I had been taken away by the Savages. She feared all she would ever see of me again would be a mutilated body, scalped and half eaten by cannibals. When the ship wrecked, she shouted to the heavens that it didn't matter a bit so long as God returned me to her, safe and sound.

"We couldn't care less about the ship! We couldn't care less about the wine, cider, dried meat, and sea biscuits. Just bring me back my son!"

"Hush, Delphine," Barbier's wife had urged her. "There's talk of sabotage as it is, what with all this quarrelling between our men. If you don't want to end up in the dock…"

But as she said it, Barbier's wife gave Mom a funny look. Or at least that's what Isabelle Talon says.

"I heard her say, 'I wouldn't put it past that damn widow to have made a pact with the devil to get her son back,'" says Mrs. Talon. "I laughed at her and she called me a witch too."

"She's such a hateful woman," Lucien Talon replies.

When the ship wrecked, Mom wasn't able to save our few belongings, our only memories of Armand. Instead she devoted her energy to gathering up what she would need to make me a ball of birthday cake. To celebrate my return (if I ever returned) and my birthday.

"You're not going to eat it?"

Her question draws me out of my thoughts. I'm still holding her gift. I stare at it without moving.

"I've never... had cake."

"I know," Mom gasps, still fighting back tears. "I wanted to give you something to remember."

I smile at her to show I'm grateful. Right beside us, the Talon brothers are looking on enviously. Madeleine is more brazen and is resting her elbows on my knee in the hopes that I'll let her have a bite. I look around for Marie-Élisabeth. I find her still off to one side, staring at the wreck. Her mind far from us.

I want to give her a piece of... *all of* my cake, just to see her smile again.

Marie-Élisabeth.

"Eat," Mom insists, beginning to worry I don't like my gift.

I bring the ball of flour, grease, and sugar to my lips and sink my teeth into it. An unreal sensation washes over my mouth. I've never felt anything like it. It's not a flavour: it's an emotion. It's palpable. It takes my tongue by storm, my palate, head, nose, ears... then my eyes.

I burst into tears without warning. I groan, but with pleasure, not distress.

I'm thirteen years old, I'm a man, I hope to marry Marie-Élisabeth... and I'm crying like a baby as I eat my very first piece of cake.

16

DON'T BLASPHEME

The slap of the water against the wood of *L'Aimable*, the crack of rigging snapping, the whistling as a piece of rope gives way. This mournful melody reminds us of its grim fate. And the wind is relentless along this coastline. The wreck will not stay still. It moves all the time. Not a lot, but all the time. The wind and the waves jostle it. Moving about on it and handling heavy crates quickly becomes a risky undertaking. Soldiers, passengers, and sailors are exhausted. At the end of the day, the drudgery comes to an end.

"We can't bring everything ashore with so few boats," Lucien Talon announces, dropping down onto the grass beside his wife. A rowboat has been destroyed, scuppered not by the Indians, according to Mr. Joutel, but by our own men.

"Many also say the shipwreck was no accident," adds Isabelle Talon.

I don't like to hear talk of the disagreements that make the adults seem like immature children in my eyes. So I leave my mom, the Talons, and the passengers around the fire to go over to Marie-Élisabeth.

As is her habit, my friend is sitting on a rock off to the side. She's sorting corn grains salvaged from the wreck, putting aside those that look rotten. Or at least that's what she was doing before the darkness forced her to stop. Now she's staring up at the thin crescent moon that is following the sun up and over the hills to the west.

"Would you like some water?" I ask, just for something to say, as I sit down beside her.

"No."

She doesn't look at me. I look at her little nose, on a face that's been redrawn by the fires off in the distance. She's sitting slightly lower than I am, but our eyes are at the same height.

"Have I done something to upset you, Marie-Élisabeth?"

"No."

Her voice is cold, neutral. Not especially aggressive, but there's no encouragement for me to continue either. I persevere.

"You're not like you used to be, Marie-Élisabeth."

She doesn't reply, doesn't even move.

"Not just with me, with everyone," I continue. "You—"

"You're just like my parents. Do you think I should be jumping for joy, too?" she interrupts, turning to face me. "Do you think I should be thanking God every day for being alive? Despite our situation?"

"Don't blaspheme."

"I'm not blaspheming. But I have the right not to like the life we're leading. I have the right not to like the state we find ourselves in, the people we're with…"

"You don't like being with me anymore?"

She looks at me for a moment, sighs, and stares off into the distance.

"I don't mean you," she whispers at last, more gently.

"You mean the others? The sailors? The soldiers? Hiens?"

I can see the muscles in her jaw stiffen.

"Don't say a word about that monster!" she hisses, spit bubbling between her lips.

"I'll never betray our secret."

I can see her jawbone relaxing now. The tendons in her neck loosen, her shoulders sink... She's calming down. For a few wordless seconds, we watch the pale glow of the sky as a flock of pelicans, stuffed full and heavy, looks for a quiet inlet in which to spend the night.

Once again, it's me who breaks the silence.

"Will you marry me, Marie-Élisabeth? The day I ask your dad for your hand, would you like to get married?"

"We're still too young, Stache."

"I'm thirteen. You'll be eleven soon enough. We're not kids anymore. And we're the best friends in the world."

She shrugs, indifferent to the question—or trying hard to look like it.

"Will you marry me, Marie-Élisabeth?"

Her expression is a strange mix of apprehension and curiosity. Maybe she's also wondering if she could marry someone who's smaller than she is.

"What do married people do, Stache? What does a husband make his wife do?"

"I don't understand."

"The other night, I was lying near my mom and dad. They thought I was asleep. I saw them in the moonlight, him on top of her. I saw them moving. I know what they were doing."

She looks at me. The fires all around have turned the blues of her eyes a shade of brick red.

"Daddy was breathing heavily, Mom was moaning," she says.

"I don't understand."

"What my mom was going through didn't seem much different to my attack."

I don't say a thing. I don't know what adults get up to between themselves. My mom has never spoken to me about that kind of thing. Maybe if Dad were still alive, he would have... but, well.

Sometimes with my friends back in La Rochelle, we would tell each other dirty stuff. They said that to make babies... Anyway, it was stupid... There's no way.

At the same time, sometimes funny stuff happens to me. Down below, I mean. Especially when I see the pretty Native girls. Especially if they're naked. Maybe Mr. Talon can explain it to me.

The more I think about it, the more I'm sure I'd be too shy to ask about anything like that. I'll listen out to what the sailors are saying instead. They're always talking about it. I always rushed away because I think—or at least I thought until now—it was a sin. Maybe if I listen to find out more, try to understand. Just listening can't be forbidden by God.

Tell you what, I'll ask the Recollects. They'll be able to tell me what I need to know. Which longings come from the Devil, for instance, and the things we need for... for married life.

"Stache?"

I give a little start, because my thoughts had wandered from Marie-Élisabeth. I realize she's still staring at me with her brick red eyes.

"If you become my husband, Stache, will you make me do what that German freebooter makes me do?"

17

THE CROCODILE

We continue unloading materials from *L'Aimable* onto the shore, where we will either transfer as much of it as possible into the hold of *Le Joly* or build a fort. If we do build a fort, we'll wait until the scouts confirm that we're in the Mississippi Delta.

"Look out! A crocodile!" a sailor shouts from the rowboat.

I don't see a thing, but he's pointing in my direction.

I'm carrying a big box that's full of knives of all sizes. Well, they're mostly on the small side since Mr. De La Salle brought them along to trade with the Natives. Two steps behind me—and down below since we're walking back up the bank that leads down to the river—Mr. Talon and Jean L'Archevêque are struggling with a heavy trunk and two young volunteers are herding eight pigs ahead of them.

"Crocodile!" a woman repeats, fifty feet away on the shore.

I still can't make out a thing when suddenly the two young boys with the pigs run off in different directions. Lucien Talon and L'Archevêque drop what they're carrying and race to the top of the slope. They run past me and to my right, clambering up a ladder formed by the rocks. An enormous spray of water spurts up from the weeds in the water just opposite me. A dark mass rears up amidst the pigs.

Just as I recognize the crocodile's silhouette, its enormous mouth belches out water like an overturned barrel. I've barely had time to step back when deafening squeals join the crashing sound of water. Two pigs—both at the same time—are imprisoned by a double row of teeth that gleam like spears.

The huge monster moves off, taking his prey with him. One of them puts up such a fight that, before the predator has disappeared back to the depths of the river, the pig tumbles back out onto the sand. But it's spurting blood from a long gash running down from its shoulder to the leg. It squeals louder than ever, thrashing to get away from the water.

I race over to pick it up.

"Leave it! Let it be!"

Lucien Talon can't see the crocodile moving off with the other pig, but I can. I can see it in the distance, carrying off its kill in its mouth. It eventually slips into the murky water, disappearing behind the mud stirred up by the attack.

"Leave the pig!" Marie-Élisabeth's father shouts as he draws closer.

"There's no danger, Mr. Talon!" I say, bending down over the poor animal that's covering the beach with its blood.

I grab it by the foot and drag it through the grass at the foot of the slope.

"Confound it, Eustache! Don't risk your life over a pig!" he rebukes me as he draws level.

"The crocodile's over there," I gasp, pointing at where I last saw it. "I wasn't in any danger."

"And that's one more animal for supper," L'Archevêque chimes in, grabbing another foot to help me haul the pig up beyond the bank. "We'll have to salvage all the blood it's losing, though. Hey! You over there! Yes, you. Bring us that pail, would you? And be quick about it!"

"Very well, what's done is done," says Lucien Talon. "We may as well bleed him completely now."

A ship's boy approaches with a metal container filled with nails. L'Archevêque empties it out and gives it a quick rinse in the water.

"I have it," he says, holding the animal up by its hind feet.

The poor animal squeals even more as it struggles, thrashing against the bucket with its head and knocking it over. The ship's boy sets the container back up, while Marie-Élisabeth's dad grabs one of the pig's ears and limbs to restrict its movements.

"Cut its throat!" he shouts to me.

"Huh? Me?"

"You're a man now, aren't you? Go on, go ahead. Kill the pig."

"B... But..."

"Let's not take all day!" grumbles L'Archevêque. "This damned pig is bleeding all over me. Slit its throat and we can fill the blasted pail!"

"With what?"

"How many knives do you have in that box you were carrying? Put one of them to good use, tarnation!"

The bad language—and Lucien Talon's slightly mocking expression—have their effect. I lean down over the little trunk I'd left on the ground and grab one of the longer cleavers. As I walk toward the pig—still trying to slip away from the four hands holding it back—I know I can't hesitate. I know that if I wait too long, the animal will get away from the men, but I'll be the laughing stock. Not them.

As the animal squeals in pain, I grab the far ear to get a better look at its throat. I thrust the knife out in front of me. The flesh opens and more blood spurts out. The pig lets out a cry not unlike the Talons' baby when his mother doesn't feed him quickly enough. The ship's boy rushes to put the bucket back under the red stream to waste as little blood as possible. The splashes of blood from the gash along its side gradually dry up as the animal is emptied from its throat.

The animal convulses again, goes calm, then stops moving altogether. Curious onlookers have gathered in the meantime. Moranget is one of them, always afraid that others will get more to eat than he does.

"We could have looked after the pig and kept it for days, weeks even," he grumbles to Jean L'Archevêque.

"That's right," L'Archevêque laughs, without paying much attention to Mr. De La Salle's nephew. "If you're so into butchery, dive into the river and get back the pig that crocodile just stole from us."

People try not to laugh, Moranget swears, insults are murmured, and then Lucien Talon puts his hand on my shoulder to guide me away. I'm still holding the blood-covered knife.

"How do you feel?" he asks.

"How do I...? Why?"

"I could see you'd never killed an animal in your life. Did you feel anything?"

"No, of course not," I reply without thinking. "I don't feel a thing."

I start to clean the blade with a scrap of cloth from a nearby bundle.

"That's good. I know tougher men than you who have felt remorse."

"The animal was going to die anyway. I put it out of its misery."

"True."

"And it was only a pig."

18

THE END OF *L'AIMABLE*

The following day, on February 21, 1685, the waves pick up and *L'Aimable*, squealing like a stuck pig, is finished off. There was still a lot to be carried off it—flour, wine, brandy, dried meat and vegetables, cloth, and musket powder—but all is lost to an indifferent sea.

"Can it be that a few jealous men or—worse!—enemies of the kingdom are sabotaging our efforts?"

No one pays me any attention when Mr. De La Salle asks the question of his closest advisers. It's not that I'm too small—come on!—just that I'm quiet and easily forgotten.

"I strongly suspect Captain Beaujeu," replies one.

"He has been jealous of your authority from the very beginning," adds another. "And he takes umbrage at your privileges."

"Many of Captain Beaujeu's supporters will take it to be an insult, indeed a provocation, that we are even suspecting him," remarks the ever-diplomatic Henri Joutel. "We have already become two rival factions. We will succumb to infighting unless we are careful. And that will be of no benefit to the colony."

"It was the Savages, not our own men, who sabotaged *L'Aimable*!"

The rumour quickly spreads across our makeshift camp as soon as furious soldiers arrive from the other side of the river.

"We saw that damned tattooed lot with Normandy blankets and bundles of cloth we didn't have time to bring ashore," shouts a man from Gascony with his thick local accent.

"I even saw them paddling out in two canoes, picking up anything they could find floating on the waves. That's our property bobbing around out there, as well they know."

I'm beginning to wonder if people aren't making too much of the incident on purpose. Might one of us, having seen the rival factions forming, have decided to invent a common enemy?

"Why not use the situation to get our hands on canoes, corn, and other foodstuffs?" suggests a Recollect. "Since the Indians have already carried off some of our belongings, why not ask for what we need in return? They'll be glad to get off lightly in order to stay on our good side."

De La Salle puts a hand to his chin, raising a questioning eyebrow aimed at Joutel.

"I think that's an excellent idea," Joutel replies. "It will create a bond between our men without turning the Indians against us."

"Very well. Would you like to take charge of the mission, Henri? You—"

"Uncle," Moranget cuts in. "I would like to be your ambassador and ask the Indians for the equivalent of what we consider to be fair for our loss."

"I require flawless diplomacy, Crevel. I fear your fiery character might not be entirely suitable."

"You can trust me, Uncle. I know how to be conciliatory."

"Not too conciliatory either," objects an officer. "Otherwise the Savages will think they can take what they want without having to negotiate or ask us first."

"In that case," Moranget replies, "I can be conciliatory... and firm."

"And flawless," repeats De La Salle.

"Of course."

Moranget, armed with the fine arquebus he always lavishes with attention, sets off in the direction of the Native village with a few men.

It is the morning of March 5, 1685. This is the date Mr. Joutel pronounced as he took notes in the book that follows him everywhere. Mom and I hear him as we move off to a quiet corner to pray. This is the time when, every time we get a chance, we kneel down to honour the memory of my brother and my father. For a few weeks now, this routine has become less of a chore for two reasons. First, I enjoy sharing my apprehensions and melancholy with Armand. And second, Mom has stopped bursting into tears at the end of the prayer. She is growing used to their absence. Proof that all sorrows end up diluted in the concerns of everyday life.

After a quarter of an hour, when we return to the centre of the camp, I spot an iguana warming itself in the sun. It's sitting on a rock, hidden in the tall grass.

"I just need a big stone," I say, taking my slingshot from my pocket and scanning the ground around me. "Right there!"

"Leave the poor animal alone, Eustache. Lizard meat is disgusting."

"But I know two sailors who'll give me a good price, Mom," I reply, creeping up on the reptile, which is becoming more nervous by the second.

"If that's what you want," she says, walking away.

I wait for her to move off, which helps calm the iguana. I begin to spin my slingshot, hoping the animal will stay still for just another seco—

"Drat!"

Just as I'm about to launch my stone, a rustling in the bushes beside us scares the animal off once and for all. Someone is walking past. The reptile dives down off its rock and I lose sight of it. I groan with disgust and let my weapon fall to my side. I turn to see the silhouette that couldn't have appeared at a worse time and to my surprise I recognize the girl I love.

"Hey! Marie-Élisabeth!"

She gives a start as she sees me. Her mind was clearly somewhere else. I pretend to laugh and try to tease her a little.

"And what are you doing there? You just made me miss out on the finest iguana you've ever seen! I'm sure I'd have gotten four or five *deniers* for it."

Instead of returning my smile or saying hello, she turns and walks away as fast as she can.

"Mar… Marie-Élisabeth! I was only joking. Marie…"

What's gotten into her?

I'm about to run after her when another movement catches my attention. I'm surprised to see Hiens, the German freebooter, come out of the very same spot.

He nods at me, spits into the bushes, then walks off, buttoning up his pants as he goes.

19

SEPARATION

I'm taking nails out of the broken boards recovered from the wreck of *L'Aimable* with Lucien Talon and Henri Joutel. When we hear the distant echo of arquebuses, Mr. Joutel doesn't even stop what he's doing to mutter: "That desperado Moranget just can't help himself with the Indians, eh?"

"Do— Do you really think so, sir?" Marie-Élisabeth's dad stammers. "Why then it's a disaster."

"I knew it was coming. Moranget is a capable soldier, but he's violent and reckless, too. He needs to be kept in check. Mr. De La Salle gives him too much of a free hand."

A Recollect catches up to us, his frock up over his ankles as he makes his way through a patch of thistles.

"Lord Jesus! Our men are in danger," he says to Henri Joutel.

"The soldiers and officers under the orders of Captain Beaujeu are gathering over there!" shouts a sailor. "Look!"

"Don't do that!" shouts De La Salle in the distance. "No reprisals, no attacks! Adopt a defensive position, no more. We shall wait for our men to return."

"If they return," Henri Joutel murmurs.

But they do come back. Although not before an hour has passed. Moranget and two of his soldiers—one of whom is seriously wounded—reappear, looking both pathetic and angry. They are furious at the Savages.

"The wretches killed two of our men!"

"They had the insolence to haggle over what they stole from us."

"We had to order them to compensate us."

"They accused us of kidnapping, tying up, and slitting the throats of up to three of their warriors."

"But we weren't taken in by their lies."

"They were very aggressive."

"We had to defend ourselves."

Mr. De La Salle is not harsh enough with his nephew for many people's liking. His actions have, after all, put the whole colony in danger from the Natives. I sense the disapproval when I head over to Jean L'Archevêque with two moorhens I've just killed for him. He had promised me a farthing for them. His circle of friends—the Duhaut brothers, a man by the name of Liotot... and the freebooter Hiens—are chatting with each other, without paying me the slightest bit of attention, as usual. To be honest, I'm not sure they even notice me.

"That swine Moranget needs a musket ball to the head," complains the older Duhaut brother.

"Last night I dreamt I planted my axe in that thick skull of his," laughs Liotot. "I've never slept as well. And if I ever get the chance, I wouldn't think twice about—"

"Keep your voice down!" one of the Duhauts interrupts. "We have an onlooker."

He nods in my direction, then continues chatting with his brother.

"Isn't that the little moron that hit you with the pulley?"

Pierre Duhaut turns his hard-as-nails face around to look at me. There's contempt in his glare, but less than I was expecting.

"It is the same miserable little wretch. But he was springing to the defence of his sweetheart, after all. He might have the muscles of a mollusc, but at least he's brave. And I'm sure he knows when to hold his tongue, doesn't he? He wouldn't like anyone to grab hold of his mother, would he? And my word, she's a fine-looking woman!"

When I hear the veiled threat about my mom, I stand as tall as I can. I hunt around in my head for a suitable reply, one that will persuade this miserable lot never to lay a hand on my mom. An ultimatum with threats of retaliation? A plea to show leniency toward a poor widow? The sobs of an orphan who also lost his little brother? But nothing seems right. Strangely enough, it's Hiens who comes to my rescue.

"No need to threaten the boy or bother the mother," he says, giving me a look that's impossible to pin down. "He'll know to keep his tongue. Especially since we haven't done a thing. We're just venting our frustrations, that's all."

The younger Duhaut brother continues to look me up and down for a moment with a mix of suspicion and menace, but the others quickly lose interest. Jean L'Archevêque ruffles my hair as he takes the moorhens. I grunt my displeasure and pluck the farthing out of his other hand.

When I turn my back on the group to walk away, I can hear Hiens with his thick German accent.

"He's no snitch," he says. "He won't go shooting his mouth off. I've already seen for myself how discreet he can be."

✑

By mid-March, the two rival factions on our expedition are now completely separate. Infighting hasn't broken out as Henri Joutel once feared, but more than one hundred of us have decided to return to France on *Le Joly*.

"Captain Beaujeu will tell the king what a failure our mission was," says a distraught Recollect. "May God forgive him his lies."

"He claims we will never find the mouth of the Mississippi," worries a second priest.

"Wait till you see the look on his face next year, when we send back a report from a thriving colony right in the heart of the territories the Spanish lay claim to," scoffs Moranget.

In the meantime, I can see Mr. De La Salle in the distance, along with Henri Joutel and the marquis de La Sablonnière, trying to convince the soldiers to keep their oath. We need them more than ever now to defend us from the hostile Natives. But, alas, the slanders and malicious gossip surrounding Mr. De La Salle have done their work: the insurgents can no longer be persuaded to stay.

"Perhaps that's why the ship was sabotaged," suggests one of De La Salle's lackeys. "Lose enough food and use that as an excuse to return home."

Being separated from one third of our group might have been cause for celebration had it included the most rotten elements. But unfortunately that's not the case. Upstanding men—officers, royal soldiers, and tradesmen—are leaving on *Le Joly*, but hardworking men too, who have had their ambition cooled. Some families—vital to the colony's survival—leave too, including women and children. The desperadoes remain, like the Duhaut brothers and L'Archevêque,

Hiens the freebooter, Liotot, Moranget, and others, not to mention all the incomp... all the less competent workers, let's say. If poor Mom is still looking to find a man to marry, she must be sorely disappointed. But, of course, this is the type of thing she and I never discuss.

Fortunately for the colony, the Talon family and six adult women are staying, my mother among them. Apart from Isabelle Talon, only one is married: Barbier's wife. The couple were keen to continue the adventure together.

We're even happier because she's pregnant. Although that's still a source of conflict: Barbier's wife has her eye on the royal privileges the Talons have already laid claim to for little Robert, who was born at sea.

"We hadn't reached our destination," the Barbier woman repeats, "which means that the boy didn't come into this world in the colony. The seigneury promised by His Majesty belongs to the child I will have."

Mr. De La Salle's problems aren't over, by the sound of things.

PART IV

Royal Land

20

HUNTING
FOR THE MISSISSIPPI

There has still been no official sighting of the mouth of the Mississippi, but the soldiers have gone, only half the ships we set off with remain, and the Native tribes are growing increasingly hostile, so Mr. de La Salle has decided to build a fort using debris from *L'Aimable*. We shall call it Fort Saint Louis.

I have work to do, but whenever I get the chance I try hard to follow Marie-Élisabeth around without her knowing. It didn't take me long to discover that unknown to her parents, two or three times a week whenever she goes to pick vegetables or wash clothes by the river, she hides away. She hides either in the tall grass in a meadow beside our camp, in a kind of cave created by a huge overhanging rock, or in a thicket of pine trees a little further away. I would worry for her safety because of the threat from the Natives... if Hiens weren't with her each time.

I know what's going on between them for the quarter of an hour they spend hidden away together. I might even feel jealous. But I know all too well that Marie-Élisabeth derives no pleasure from these secret encounters. If she did, she would be glowing every time she walked back from them. But more often than not she's crying. Or in a rage. Or her face is impossible to read.

How is the freebooter holding her in his power like this? How is he convincing her to give herself to him?

I don't know what to do. I don't know if I should speak to Mr. Talon about it. I'm worried about what might happen. But I don't think I'm helping Marie-Élisabeth by continuing to keep the promise I made her. Keeping quiet about what I know no longer seems the right thing to do. But at the same time, who should I talk to? A Recollect priest? Henri Joutel? And how would Hiens react if he found himself accused of repeatedly raping an eleven-year-old girl? Wouldn't he take revenge on us? Or wouldn't the monsters that he hangs around with?

Fort Saint Louis is quickly taking shape. It must be said that it's not particularly sophisticated. We put up the main building at the top of a mound that would make an attack by the Natives more difficult—but not impossible. Mr. De La Salle lives there along with a few lucky men from his entourage and the Recollect priests. Then there's a house for the women and children, two more for the soldiers and workers, a stable, a warehouse, and a chapel next to our leaders' central building.

But these buildings of mud, straw, and fodder aren't enough to house everyone. Some men are building huts out of buffalo pelts to shelter from the bad weather.

Sentries guard the four corners of our fort at all times. They have orders to shoot any Natives on sight. Everyone is gripped by fear.

After *Le Joly* left with at least one hundred twenty settlers who were hostile to Mr. De La Salle, we might have thought that peace would settle over those of us left behind. No such luck! Because of our precarious predicament and the constant threats we face, discontent is growing.

For heaven's sake! Why can't some people get it into their heads that we'll first have to roll up our sleeves and work hard before things improve?

"We captured the deserters, sir."

Henri Joutel presents René-Robert Cavelier de La Salle with two men who fled the fort to strike out alone. They are pitiful. Their week-long stay in the forest has tested them to the limit. They are filthy, famished, thirsty, exhausted, and covered in mosquito bites.

Perhaps they wanted to go live with the Natives. One of them has fallen in love with a Native girl, I hear. Perhaps they reckoned on finding the Mississippi themselves, and planned on heading up it to the Canadian colonies before taking the first ship back to France. No one explains what they were thinking to us. They are tried behind closed doors.

"The verdict is in!" Moranget declares as he sits down among us that same evening by the fire. "The ringleader will be hanged tomorrow for desertion. Right there on that tree. You'll all be here to see it—a reminder of the fate that awaits traitors working against His Majesty's will. The second deserter has wholeheartedly repented and our leaders have chosen to be lenient. Nonetheless, he will have to sign an agreement to serve the king, right here in this very land, for ten years."

"Time we left once and for all and started looking for this Mississippi everyone's talking about," a man murmurs a little too loudly.

"And so we shall!" Moranget declares, for once not flying into a rage whenever he hears someone say what Mr. De La Salle should do.

He's no doubt thrilled at the thought of watching a man be executed tomorrow; he hardly ever puts his hand on the shoulder of the person he's talking to. He seems to be in top form all right.

"Any man who, like you, wants to see some action will soon be in his element," he continues. "Our leader has asked me to inform you that in a few days some fifty of us will be leaving Fort Saint Louis for *La Belle*. We will sail along the river until we find the Mississippi Delta and can at last begin our great sacred mission."

The shouts that greet the announcement seem to me to be more relieved than happy. I am hoping for only one thing: that Hiens the monster is not one of the men left behind at the fort. Or any of the thugs he hangs around with.

For once, God answers my prayers. Or maybe it's my little brother the angel that I now pray to every day. Either way. When Mr. De La Salle leaves Fort Saint Louis with fifty men in five canoes to meet up with *La Belle*, the dastardly Hiens, Duhaut, Liotot, and L'Archevêque go with him.

Marie-Élisabeth's attitude completely changes from one day to the next. Without turning back into the cheerful little girl she was before, she begins to smile again and use sentences more than three words long. We can all feel how much calmer she is. If ever I needed proof that the time she spent with Hiens was against her will, now I have it.

Lucien and Isabelle Talon, without really understanding why their daughter has been so completely transformed—"It must be puberty," he father suggests—are delighted to see her smiling again and showering her younger siblings with affection.

"She had her first period," her mother agrees. "It's bound to be playing a part. I explained to her that—Oh! You're still here, Eustache. I thought that you'd gone back to Delphine."

Even those closest to me sometimes manage not to notice me.

And so we spend quite a nice spring together, even though life at Fort Saint Louis isn't easy. We need to till the soil to grow crops, and Henri Joutel is set on improving our makeshift buildings. I'm appointed to help build an oven away from our quarters.

"Joutel is scared of fire," a cook grumbles. "He should be more worried about those Indians killing a poor old baker all by himself away from the fort."

Weeks pass with no news of Mr. De La Salle.

"He must have found his river and headed up it," ventures a man by the fire one night.

"Or he's dead, killed by the Savages," says another.

"If he did, De La Salle must be halfway to Europe by now, with us stuck here," says a third.

"No way, birdbrain. This colony idea is his dream, his—"

"Yeah, yeah, his utopia. De La Salle's a madman, a crank. You don't need to be one of those Indian witch doctors to see that."

"Ssh! You'll hang if Moranget hears you."

"Let *him* hang! His uncle's mad. I'll say it and I'll say it again."

"Then why don't you go tell Henri Joutel?" asks Lucien Talon. He's not serious, but his voice is as calm as ever. "He'll be overjoyed to hear everything we've done has been in vain and that we should all take the next boat back to France."

People laugh, but there's grumbling, too. Everyone knows we're off to a bad start, and some have lost faith. And I must admit that the more I understand what's at stake here, the more I find out about the problems we face, the more I too feel like giving into discouragement. But whenever I look at Mom and see the tiny flicker of hope in her eyes that keeps her going, that works hard to convince her we didn't leave behind her world of beggars for nothing, that tells her we're trying to build a new life and a happy future, well, then I take a step back. I think to myself that I have no right to destroy the only thing that helps her put up with our fate, that allows her not to feel guilty about dragging me all the way across the ocean and into the dream of an explorer who has—perhaps—lost his mind.

Out of love for my mother, out of the friendship we have with the Talon family, out of my love for Marie-Élisabeth, I want to believe in a French colony in America.

I want to believe in Fort Saint Louis, Louisiana, and René-Robert Cavelier De La Salle.

21

SAVAGES AND A SNAKE

"Indians! Indians! The Indians are attacking!"

The alarm is sounded early enough for us to take refuge inside the fort. When I go over to Mom, she's one of the volunteers wetting the roofs of our homes with buckets of water. In case of flaming arrows. But a few shots later, the threat has passed. The Natives weren't too set on war today.

"Where's the Big Man?"

The former helmsman of *L'Aimable*, who had preferred to continue on the adventure with us rather than go back with Beaujeu, had been right behind me three minutes ago.

"He was with me," I tell Barbier. "We were out at the oven and—"

I don't finish what I'm saying. Instead I run out of the fort.

"Eustaaaache!" shouts my mom behind me.

"Wait!" Barbier cries after me. "There might be more Indians close by! Come back!"

I pretend not to hear.

"Staaaache!"

Even Marie-Élisabeth can't stop me... although it's so great to hear the concern in her voice!

I'm very fond of the Big Man. He's never treated me like a kid. He put up with me beside him the whole time when he was at the helm of *L'Aimable*. If he's in danger, I want to be the first to help.

"Eus... Eustache..."

"Big Man!"

The helmsman is sprawled on the ground, half in the grass and half on the sand. His skinny legs, mixed in among the grass, make him look even scrawnier than usual. I lean over him. The first thing I look for is the wound. Where did they get him? Was it an arrow or a—

"Look out!"

I barely have time to straighten up before a huge rattlesnake springs out from beneath a stone. Its fangs, still glistening with venom, brush my face. Then, a second later, it turns away from me and slithers back into the grass. It disappears like a crocodile sliding into a river. I can see the crocodile in my mind for a moment and the similarities between both attacks send shivers down my spine.

"The swine bit me," moans the Big Man. "Right there, on my foot."

I don't waste a second examining the wound that I can now see at last: a red cut that seems harmless enough.

"Those devilish creatures are deadlier than a volley of Indian arrows," says a Recollect behind me, a man not renowned for his tact.

Beside him stand four fusiliers, nervously pointing their weapons in all directions. Barbier and Moranget arrive too, looking appropriately alarmed.

"Will I die, Father? Will I die?" the Big Man asks.

"It's possible," the Recollect replies, blessing the helmsman, while Barbier and Moranget lean in to grab him by
the shoulders.

"Of course you won't!" I blurt out, turning to glare at the
priest. "We know the Indian remedies. They've already pro-
ven their worth."

"On whom?" asks the Recollect, genuinely surprised.

What an idiot!

But before I can find a reply to comfort the Big Man, he
cries out in pain. Barbier and Moranget are hauling him off
to the fort.

The helmsman, after several days of fever and gangrene,
succumbs to the venom. He dies to widespread distress,
liked by all. We bury his remains in a little cemetery nearby.
Then, on the same day, a fisherman drowns within shouting
distance of our wharf.

"Do you think we're all going to die here, Stache?" Marie-
Élisabeth asks me, one night when she's particularly
talkative.

We're walking along the path that links the women's
quarters to the depot and the chapel. We've just delivered
the candles the Recollects had been asking for. We'd had
to trim them since the candlesticks had been too narrow.
The leftover wax was wrapped in a piece of cloth and now
we're carrying it carefully back to the storehouse.

"Of course we're all going to die here!"

The answer surprises my friend and she turns to face me.

"Are you serious?"

"More than serious. Only it won't be for another fifty years, as part of a prosperous colony, envied by everyone in Canada."

She laughs. Or rather, she stretches back her lips, revealing her pretty teeth, which hasn't happened in months. For her, that's the equivalent of a guffaw. We walk on for a little while, and then she asks:

"Will we have children, Stache?"

I'm so taken aback by her question that I stop dead in the middle of the trail. At the same moment, a shooting star, right opposite me against the pink of the setting sun, traces the curve of a raised eyebrow.

"We'll have... If God answers my prayers, Marie-Élisabeth, we'll have more children than your parents."

I get another chance to admire her teeth as her fingers curl around my wrist. I resist the temptation to throw away the wax I'm carrying to take her hand in mine. Her shoulder snuggles in under my arm and I breathe in the dry smell of her hair as her locks brush against my face.

My heart takes flight. My head spins, drowning the world in its pain and uncertainty. In a flash, I feel in control of my life and our destiny. I tell myself that no drownings, no explorers, no Natives, and definitely no German freebooters will ever jeopardize happiness and hope of such intensity.

I don't know it yet, but this is the only moment of true bliss I'll ever have with Marie-Élisabeth.

22

THE NEW FORT

"Mr. De La Salle has sent me to find settlers to build a new fort!" announces a man by the name of Villeperdry.

He's just arrived with a small group of men. Everyone in Fort Saint Louis has gathered around them. We're in the sweltering heat of June, at the height of the fledgling season. Black-crested titmice, warblers, orioles, and green jays fly overhead, streaking the sky and the leaves around us in a frenzy of colour.

"A new one?" asks Henri Joutel, who has worked so hard to make the current fort fit to live in.

"Yes, sir," replies Villeperdry. "Mr. De La Salle would like you to maintain a bridgehead here with thirty men or so, but Mr. Moranget is to follow us with all the others, women and children included."

"But you only have two canoes!" Moranget points out. "There will be eighty of us making the trip."

"You will have to come by land, sir," explains Villeperdry. "On foot."

"The mouth of the Mississippi isn't far then!" says Joutel, thrilled.

"Twenty leagues away, sir."

"Twenty leagues?!"

Moranget almost shouts the words.

"With Mrs. Talon and her infant child?" he goes on, still almost shouting. "With the pregnant Mrs. Barbier? With a handful of kids under ten? Why ever didn't my uncle send *La Belle*?"

"With respect, sir, your uncle is increasingly severe concerning our conditions. A number of us have died from exhaustion. We would appreciate it if you came. Perhaps you will have him listen to reason."

I turn instinctively toward Mom. Her sad smile doesn't fool me: she's disappointed. I think that, despite its harshness, she has become attached to the life we lead at Fort Saint Louis. The chores have given meaning to her life. Same goes for the hope that has come from being in Louisiana. Leaving here for somewhere else where we'll have to start all over again will require energy that she'll have to dig deep to find.

"It'll be great, Mom," I say, trying to sound enthusiastic. "The real Louisiana at last. We can wave goodbye to here— it's been tough going since the start."

I look over at Isabelle Talon (as demoralized as my mom), Lucien Talon (teeth gritted), then Marie-Élisabeth. Her shattered expression brings me back to a reality I had lost sight of: being reunited with the other members of the colony also means living alongside Hiens the freebooter and his band of demons.

For days and nights, among the mosquitoes, snakes, and the constant threat posed by crocodiles, we march around lakes, marshes, and swampland. The women have trouble with their skirts and the priests struggle as their cassocks catch on prickly shrubs and bushes. Exhausted children seek refuge on the shoulders of the strongest men.

"This stagnant water is blowing the putrid breath of disease all over us," a priest worries.

"Damn De La Salle! May his soul burn in hell!" a second Recollect replies.

Fortunately, Moranget is too far ahead to hear, or else the priest would now be swimming with the frogs.

"Are you OK, Marie-Élisabeth?"

"I'm OK, Stache."

She scratches the side of her head. Her temples and forehead are swollen with insect bites. Her greasy hair, pulled into a braid, hangs heavily around her neck.

"Two or three more days," says Lucien Talon as he catches up to us, "and we'll be there. Villeperdry just told me."

Madeleine, her tiny legs dangling in front of her father's chest, is half asleep, resting a cheek against his head.

"Only two or three more days," he says again, before striding on toward his wife.

It takes us five more days to at last reach the new fort. It's also called Saint Louis. Like the one before. We assume that if Mr. De La Salle gives it the same name, it's because the second one will be the *real* fort, the first nothing but a rough sketch, unworthy of our great mission.

Our disappointment is in proportion to these expectations… and to our exhaustion.

✑

"Welcome, my friends! Welcome!" cries René-Robert Cavelier de La Salle as the first of us arrive.

His warm approach—more jovial than is his custom—is no doubt designed to mask the surrounding desolation. The only building is nothing but a series of stakes arranged in a square and covered with animal hide. It contains a few kegs of brandy and powder. That's all.

As for the rest of it, the men have built themselves makeshift shelters from fodder and straw, across a treeless piece of land overrun with weeds. The closest forest is one league inland.

"Where are we going to get the wood to build the fort?" wonders Lucien Talon in a low voice. "Why set up the colony here? And why send for us now, with the women and children in tow, when nothing is ready yet?"

We're at the top of a slope from where we can see the vast grassy plains stretching out all around. We also look down over a big marsh that's home to an impressive gathering of curlews, turkey fowl, geese, thrushes, plovers, and other birdlife. And a broad river sets waves rolling off toward a bay.

"We shall call it Saint Louis Bay," trumpets De La Salle. "And the river shall be *Rivière aux bœufs*: Buffalo River. It's the perfect name: there are buffalo everywhere. We'll eat our fill every day."

Heads nod approvingly.

Out on the water we can see the calm, indifferent silhouette of *La Belle*. The summer sun is suffocating. Mom holds me tight against her. When I half turn to put my hand around her too, I notice something I haven't seen until now: I'm taller than she is!

I've grown.

Despite the hardships and the difficult life we lead, my body has at last answered the call of adolescence. In the space of a few weeks, I've grown to a size I thought would take me two or even three more years to reach.

That must mean that now I'm taller than Marie-Élisabeth, too. I'm with her every day and I hadn't noticed. Unless she's grown at the same rate.

I spin around to look for her... and my gaze falls on Hiens. There he is on the shore, standing with his back to the river, his feet a little apart, leaning over a fruit that he's peeling with his broken knife. His eyes, though, are trained on our group.

He's searching for Marie-Élisabeth. When I spot him, he's lifting up his head to get a better look at her. He gives a sinister smile as he greets her with the blade of his knife, holding it up in front of him.

Marie-Élisabeth turns away and pretends not to have seen him.

I forget all about wanting to compare our heights.

23

INSULTING OUR MOTHERS

Villeperdry is dead, felled by a tree as he built the fort. De La Salle barely batted an eyelid. "We have no time to feel sorry for ourselves," I heard him mutter to Moranget.

Our leader is becoming more and more demanding, making us carry heavy loads of wood from the forest to the shores of Saint Louis Bay. It's from here that the next expeditions are set to head up the Mississippi.

"If it even is the Mississippi," grumbles Jean L'Archevêque as he drops down beside us.

I'm not far away, cleaning the carcasses of two rabbits I killed with my slingshot.

While honourable, upstanding, and brave men die of exhaustion and fever, the dregs of society are beginning to make up a bigger share of the group.

"How much do you want for them?" L'Archevêque asks me, pointing a finger at the animals as I skin them.

"They're for my mother, sir. Sorry."

"And how much do you want for your mother?"

I look up so quickly it hurts my neck. It was Pierre Duhaut who said it, the older brother. He's looking at me with his bulging yellow eyes, a mocking look hovering at the edges of his mouth. His brother is sitting beside him, his hands resting on his lap, looking down at the ground. He guffaws without bothering to look up. Liotot, Hiens, and two or three others allow themselves a smile.

I fight back the urge to spit in Pierre Duhaut's face. It takes me a good second or two to regain my composure, then I take a deep breath to better control my voice.

"My mother isn't the whore that yours was, sir," I say, trying to sound calm.

The Duhaut brothers stand up in concert. I leap to my feet just as quickly to confront them. They're already eating into the ten paces that separate us, one with his fist clenched, the other rummaging around in his pockets for his knife. I'm quicker than they are, though, and I've already flung the rabbits to the ground and am spinning my slingshot. I can only hit one of them, but the threat's enough to slow them down.

L'Archevêque steps in to try to calm everyone down. He too is now on his feet, holding out an arm in front of his two companions.

"Easy now! Let's not give Moranget a reason to open a prison."

"I'm not going to let some snot-nosed kid insult my mother," barks Pierre Duhaut.

"You insulted his, didn't you?"

"I insulted no one," the younger Duhaut bristles, pretending to take another step, without taking his eyes off my whirling slingshot. "There's no way I'm going to let this little brat say that my mother is... was..."

"What's going on here?"

We turn around in surprise to see Lucien Talon standing there. We hadn't heard him coming.

"Mind your own business, carpenter!" L'Archevêque warns him. "This is between us."

"If it involves young Eustache, then it concerns me, too. That's my future son-in-law you're talking to."

My slingshot loses some of its velocity as I stare at Marie-Élisabeth's dad in amazement.

"What are you talking about?" asks L'Archevêque in surprise. "Your daughter isn't—"

"My daughter will be twelve next spring. Old enough to marry. The boy will be fourteen then, and a suitable husband. He's practically family already."

Lucien Talon's words astound only me, but they have the advantage of taking up a second or two. It's time enough for tempers to cool and, more importantly, for other settlers to take an interest in our group, including a few Recollect priests who happen to be walking by. Sensing a disagreement when they see my spinning slingshot, they draw nearer. The Duhaut brothers take a step back. They pretend to look frustrated, but they can see a way out here, a way to avoid getting on the wrong side of Moranget without losing face.

"Everything OK here?" a priest asks.

"Of course!" Lucien Talon answers cheerfully, diplomatic as ever. "Look at the two lovely rabbits these gentlemen were pretending to steal from my future son-in-law."

"Your future son-in-law? Will we have a wedding to celebrate, Lucien?" the priest asks, watching as I slide the slingshot back into the pocket of my pants.

"Next spring, Father, next spring," Talon replies, putting his arms around my shoulder and leading me away.

I slip away from him long enough to pick up my rabbits. He smiles at everyone as he waits, but I can see an agitated finger tapping nervously against the cloth of his pants.

When I get back up to follow him, I catch L'Archevêque giving him a grateful look. The Duhauts make a show of ignoring us. Liotot and the others look over in Moranget's direction, but he's too far away, off with our leaders, to have noticed the confrontation.

Only Hiens's snarl leaves me puzzled. He leers at Lucien Talon and at me in turn, and the crease that puts his mouth out of shape shows all his contempt, or perhaps even his hatred for us. The man terrifies me, partly because I can never tell what he's really feeling.

What he's really thinking.

24

THE LAME

In the fall of 1685, Mr. De La Salle decides to set off on a new voyage of exploration to ensure we are well and truly in the delta of his famous Mississippi. We might be distressed to see him go, were it not for the fact that it proves a good opportunity to calm the frenetic pace at which we have to carry heavy loads of wood from the distant forest to the top of our slope. The rate at which the fort is built slows as men become exhausted... or die.

"Mom, I want to be part of the expedition."

"You're mad! You're much too sma... too young!"

We're sharing a buffalo stew mixed in with mushrooms that Isabelle Talon picked in a dank and sticky copse.

"Mr. De La Salle needs volunteers, Mom. And I'm not so small anymore. Have you noticed I'm taller than you now?"

From the way she suddenly looks at me, I can see it's news to her.

"Me too, I wanna go too," whines Pierre Talon, who's only nine and a half. "I'm almost as big as Eustache and—"

"Stop talking nonsense," his mother interrupts, "and eat."

"But Eustache…"

"It's of no concern to you."

"Will you be part of the expedition, Mr. Talon?" I ask Marie-Élisabeth's dad. He's eating opposite me, on the other side of the fire.

"Possibly. Under Mr. Joutel's authority, only women, children, the lame, and fewer than ten soldiers will remain at the fort."

"See, Mom? I'm no longer a kid. And I'm not sick or lame. Nothing's keeping me here."

As I speak, I sneak a look in Marie-Élisabeth's direction. I hope she'll think I'm brave and will look sad to see me go. But she's not looking at us. A little off to the side, she's half-heartedly eating her stew without saying a word, her jaw clenched in a rage that doesn't ever seem to end. For weeks now, her attitude again seems to be at odds with her true nature. She is not passive and downtrodden as she was before the summer, but bad-tempered and irritable. It's another Marie-Élisabeth that neither I nor her parents know.

Once again I'd like to know if Hiens is no stranger to her condition, but not once—no matter how closely I've kept a discreet eye on them—have I surprised them together. Marie-Élisabeth spends her days with her mother and, if ever she has the chance to go off by herself—to go to the toilet, for instance, or to pick berries—I can always see the German freebooter in the fort or somewhere close by.

As I try to reassure myself, it suddenly comes to me…

What they've been doing is so simple that I'm annoyed not to have thought of it earlier.

The younger Duhaut brother has a fever and is exempted from going on the expedition. His older brother begs to stay by his side, but Moranget is having none of it. L'Archevêque, Liotot, and company also leave... but not Hiens. In a strange accident that no one was witness to, he seems to have hurt his foot.

"That rotten German has probably found a way to wolf down more food with the rest of us gone," sighs Lucien Talon as he drapes a buffalo pelt over his shoulders to protect himself from the north wind. This morning, it's blowing with the fury of January. And it's fall. It looks like we're in for a rough winter. Perhaps we'll have snow. It reminds me that Isabelle Talon promised Mom mild weather in America. What would things be like if we were in Canada?

I've been kept off the expedition. I need to take care of Mom, even though she clearly has nothing more than a cold.

I grumbled when I heard the news, but my heart wasn't in it. Deep down I'm glad not to be leaving Marie-Élisabeth behind, not with Hiens in the vicinity.

As he helps little Pierre measure the plank in front of him, Lucien Talon asks me without looking up, "Do you think Mr. Joutel's trying to do me a favour by making me stay behind at the camp?"

"Oh no, Mr. Talon!" I reply. "There are hardly any experienced workers left at the fort. Surely they need someone who can work with wood to make sure we progress with the buildings while the others are away."

"For all that I can get done alone with this band of lame men and incompetents to work with! You and my sons are my best apprentices."

I'm going to say something or other when I spot Marie-

Élisabeth in the distance, carrying a bundle of clothes over her shoulder. She's holding Madeleine's hand and walking off to a nearby stream. Instinctively, as I do every time I see her walk away, I look around for Hiens.

I find him in no time near the men's quarters, smoking a pipe. He's sitting against the outside wall, wrapped up in an ugly wool blanket. He doesn't show the slightest interest in the two girls as they walk off.

But I've guessed what he's up to. And soon I'll be able to unmask him.

Very soon.

25

THE SOUND
OF THE HUMMINGBIRD

The new Fort Saint Louis doesn't come close to even the basic comforts of the first settlement. Two crude constructions separate the men from the women and children.

To move my bed closer to the door, I pretend the smoke from the fire that warms our shelter is bothering me. Then I move back part of the door's cover until I can see outside. The sky is shining with so many stars that, even on this moonless night, it's a dazzling sight. The silhouette of the women's quarters stands out in such detail that I can make out the wisps of straw making up the roof.

And so it couldn't be easier, even though the evening fires are all put out at midnight, to make out a shadow moving across the skyline. No one but the sentries is allowed to be out walking, but as everyone—apart from Henri Joutel— knows, the watchers doze off between two pipes and so it's no trouble walking around wherever we please. I know, for instance, that sometimes the lame—or those who claim to be—sneak off to meet the Native women.

But not now.

Set against the bright light of the stars and half stooped over to try to keep out of sight, a silhouette betrays the familiar outline, the gait, and the nervous movements of Marie-Élisabeth.

I knew it! That's why, even though Hiens is back in the picture, she's stopped disappearing during the day. It's to make sure they won't be surprised again.

I drag myself out of my warm blanket, shiver for a second against the icy onslaught of the night, then move outside beneath the dizzying gulf of the too-bright sky. The hair on the rabbitskin neckwarmer I made for myself tickles my neck.

Hiding from view in grass that doesn't come past my thighs is no mean feat. There are no trees, no palisades, no rocks to swallow up our shadows—could the sentries be any worse? The hunt is on, and it's both difficult and easy: anyone can see me coming, but the same goes for Marie-Élisabeth.

I first lose sight of her when she goes over a small hill. I run as hard as I can to catch up—not easy with my legs all folded up to make myself as small as can be. I catch sight of her again as she's walking into a copse full of lush foliage. I know this jumble of weeds; there's a big flat rock in the middle of them. We've seen rattlesnakes here no fewer than three times. What a risk she's taking!

I don't dare go any further. I'd be too exposed going down the shadowless slope. Better to stay crouched down where I am. At any rate, if she passes through the copse and on toward the river, say, I'll see her easily. And I don't need to see what she's up to on the flat rock surrounded by foliage. I know only too well.

I know because I've just seen another silhouette. Hiens's. He doesn't even bother to hide. He plunges into the dark leaves, leaving a more distant path that leads to the forest.

He shows no sign of a limp.

⁓

I spend the quarter hour it takes to satisfy the German free-booter's primal urges tiptoeing my way down the hill toward the copse. Crouched down behind a clump of grass that's somewhat higher than the rest, I wait for the two conspirators to reappear.

Marie-Élisabeth gasps in surprise when I stand up as she emerges from the shadows and starts to walk up the hill. Hiens is ten paces behind her and simply stands still, legs apart in his familiar stance. I can't make out his face, but it's easy to imagine his usual sneer, both indifferent and mocking. His eyes send back the faint glow of two stars.

"What are you doing here?"

The voice of the girl promised to me is halfway between a whisper and an angry roar. I don't answer. I don't even look at her. I'm still looking at Hiens, making sure he doesn't dash in my direction to make me regret my plan.

"So you're spying on me now?" she hisses.

"I don't know why you keep meeting this swine, Marie-Élisabeth."

"That's none of your business."

I can hear the bubbles of spit rolling around between her teeth. Her irritation at seeing me is slowly turning to her usual anger. The fury that roams between her heart and her lips. The fury borne of Hiens the rapist.

"Why, Marie-Élisabeth?"

"Go away. Don't get involved."

I still don't budge. Several seconds go by with nobody speaking, nobody moving. It's the German who at last breaks the silence with his guttural accent.

"Did you hear my friend? Stay quiet, just like you've been all along."

"Do you love this man, Marie-Élisabeth? Do you sneak off to meet him because you like him?"

I'm being ironic, but at the same time I shudder to think that my sweetheart might answer yes.

She turns to Hiens for a moment, then rests her eyes on me.

"He's a piece of shit," she says simply. "But that doesn't change a thing."

"It changes everything. Tell him it's the last time you'll see him like this. Tell him you're no longer a frightened little girl, that he has no right to make you—"

"You don't understand, Stache!" she cuts in, her voice higher now. "It's not that simple. Don't play the tough guy. You're no match for him. The two inches you've grown over the past couple of months aren't going to help you lay out a killer like him."

Even from ten paces away, I can easily make out the German's muffled laughter. He puts his hand in his pocket and for a brief moment the blade he whips out hurls the flame of its murderous intentions toward me.

As though a warning sent by the light from the stars.

My spinning slingshot sounds like a hummingbird. It all seems too unreal for me to be afraid. I feel like I'm in a strange dream. Two enemies are squaring up to kill, with the sound of a hummingbird for a war cry.

"Don't do it, Stache!" Marie-Élisabeth warns me, closing her hand over my free arm. "Hurl that stone and I'll never speak to you again. And I'll never... I'll never agree to marry you."

The humming sound dies away.

"So you love him then? That much?"

"Your slingshot isn't going to help you stop a man like that from slicing you up into mortadella."

"Says who?"

Hiens's cruel laugh rings out again. Louder this time, since I can hear it above the buzzing of my slingshot. But the freebooter just stands there, no more threatening than he needs to be, apart from the blade that continues to dazzle me with stars from the end of his wrist.

"He killed the Indians, Stache. It was him."

I don't know what she's talking about and I take my eyes off the German for two seconds to turn toward her. The expression on her face is lost to me in the darkness. I only detect her fear in the slight tremble to her voice as she goes on.

"The Savages who were murdered. It led to war with the village beside where we first lived. Remember? He killed them. To show me he wasn't fooling around. That it was no big deal to him. He made me go with him and see the bodies, all covered in flies. If I don't do what he says, if I don't give in to his desires, he won't think twice about doing the same to my dad. And my mom."

"Or with your mother, lad," the freebooter adds.

He's becoming so sure of his own power that the blade of his knife is now hovering at knee height, pointed down toward the ground, no more of a threat than that. The hummingbird on the end of my arm hums louder. But instead of growing alarmed, Hiens adds, "And if ever I'm killed by some crazy fool, then Duhaut would be only too happy to have his way with the lovely Delphine."

This time, the hummingbird dies. Right there on the spot. I let the stone fall at my feet. Marie-Élisabeth's tense fingers release their hold on my arm.

"A wise decision," Hiens concludes as a streak of stars climbs up to the pocket of his pants. "Now get lost!"

I grab Marie-Élisabeth's hand.

"Come."

She gives in. Together we climb back up the hill, leaving the freebooter behind us.

Suddenly I stop. I stare at a cactus to the right. Marie-Élisabeth, rooted to the spot, starts to wriggle on the end of my arm.

"What? What are you looking at?"

"Nothing. Let's go."

We set off toward the fort again. I didn't get a good look, but I'm sure I'm not mistaken.

In the shadows of the prickly bushes, in among the plump stems, I recognized the silhouette of Lucien Talon.

He must have followed me when I left. He must have witnessed everything. Maybe he'll catch Hiens by surprise when he comes along behind us. I don't do a thing that might reveal him.

But I'm afraid. Not for Marie-Élisabeth's dad, but for Mom.

What will happen to her if Lucien Talon kills Hiens?

26

THE DISAPPEARANCE

Lucien Talon's bed looks as though someone got up without pulling up the covers and arranging his affairs. I lie down on mine and wait for him to come back.

And I wait.

As uncertain and afraid as I am, I end up falling asleep. The men stirring at dawn wake me. Lucien Talon still hasn't come back.

"The carpenter's up early this morning," a settler remarks. "Must've been in a hurry to get to work. Took his axe with him. How am I supposed to cut the firewood now?"

The taste of vomit rises in my throat. Unease grabs hold of me just as tightly as two strong arms around my chest.

"Hello, Eustache. Have you seen Lucien?"

"N… no, Mrs. Talon."

"Strange. Usually…"

She doesn't get to finish her sentence. Robert, her newborn child, is screaming for attention. Pierre grabs me around the waist, trying to haul me into the kind of affectionate wrestling match you have with an older brother—which is what I am to him. Jean-Baptiste follows his lead behind me. Ludovic, all of six years old, comes to my rescue. But my heart's not in it this morning.

Marie-Élisabeth is off with Madeleine, both carrying wooden buckets to be filled down at the river. My sweetheart, as usual, is careful not to meet my eye. Even when Madeleine blows me a kiss.

"Didn't sleep well, Eustache?" asks Mom, pecking me on the cheek. "You look a sight!"

I look all around. I look for Hiens, but I don't see him. And yet at this hour he can usually be seen smoking his first pipe by the fire, not far from the shelter.

I free myself from the boys, trying not to seem impatient, and move off in spite of myself, in spite of my foreboding, toward the path.

"Don't go too far, Eustache."

"I'm going hunting. I'll be back soon."

I quickly reach the top of the hill and the thicket of thorns where I spotted Lucien Talon. Down below, bathed in the morning mist, I can also make out the copse of love that dare not speak its name.

I scan every blade of grass, looking for a clue to help me find out what might have happened after I left. I find nothing.

I pace up and down the surrounding area in the hopes of finding a flattened patch of grass, a piece of torn clothing, perhaps even a trace of blood. Strangely enough, my anxiety increases, not upon discovering signs of a struggle, but because I remain in the dark.

I come across a series of trampled saplings, making me suspect that a man (or two) or an animal (or two) might have passed by here. The flattened path points to the river.

I start off in this direction, to reach an out-of-the-way bend along its banks. I come to a steep slope, from where it's impossible to get down to the water unless I clamber my way over uncertain rocks and prickly cactuses. Why would any animal come here?

On the shore below, a glint of light suddenly catches my eye. Between two shingles, a ray of sunshine has surged through an opening upstream to land on a piece of metal—or perhaps polished stone—making it shine like glass. I forget all about my sense for danger. Without worrying about perhaps running into a bivouac shelter belonging to the Karankawa people—the Natives from the area—I set off to satisfy my curiosity.

Halfway down, I come to a sudden stop. Off in the distance, a dark mass is floating in the river between two tree trunks. A human body? A dead buffalo? Clinging to two bushes, I strain to identify the outline. When a wave pushes against the tree trunks, the mass tips over and I can make out an arm, then a hand trying to grab hold of the branches.

Is it Lucien Talon? Hiens? There's no way to tell from this distance.

I'm wondering where I can find a ford to cross in order to help the man when the scaly outline of an enormous crocodile moves into view. In a split second, the reptile races across the water. It reaches the man and snatches him with his huge mouth. I watch them melt soundlessly into the water, the only noise coming from the music of the river.

Everything has happened so quickly that I'm still standing right there, hanging on to two bushes. When earth and sand begin to spill down over my wrists, I understand that they won't hold my weight for much longer; it's time to move on down. I reach the foot of the slope without taking my eyes off the spot where the crocodile disappeared. But from this lower angle, I can no longer see a thing.

I'm all set to follow the river back when I suddenly remember what brought me down to the water in the first place. I turn around and find the glint of sunlight that caught my eye from the top of the slope: Hiens's knife! The half-broken one with the bone handle. No doubt the same one he threatened me with.

I pick it up and gasp in horror: it's covered in blood! So the freebooter stabbed Lucien Talon. And Mr. Talon, as he lay dying, was carried off by the river and swept out to the tree trunks, where he ended up in the crocodile's mouth.

Unless...

Nothing says it's the blood of Marie-Élisabeth's dad. And even if it were, who says the wound was fatal? If the knife was lying here, perhaps it's because it was Hiens who fell into the water, Hiens who was carried off by the crocodile.

I stoop down over the water and clean the blade with the palm of my hand. I slide the weapon into my belt and retrace my steps.

My chest is puffed up with renewed hope. It's possible all right that the man I saw in the distance was Hiens. In the meantime, Lucien Talon must have returned to the fort and gone back to his family. I shouldn't spend too long here. I should get back to them. Mom must be wondering where I am anyway.

I climb back up the slope so that I don't have to walk all the way around. When I reach the top, I glance back down below. I almost cry out in surprise as I see something move on the shoreline.

His face to the ground and his body twitching nervously, a bearded man is making slow progress, scanning the ground around him. Hiens is looking for his knife.

27

DIVINE IMPOTENCE

Isabelle Talon cries over her husband's disappearance for no more than ten days. In a world as cruel and unstable as ours, we quickly resign ourselves to death. To absence. She and my mom, already close friends, become sisters in widowhood. Joutel sends men off to look for his carpenter, but they quickly conclude that he lost his way in the forest while out hunting rabbits.

I keep quiet. I pretend to look for him with the others. I'm the only one to know we'll never find the remains of this decent family man.

And so I refuse to turn Hiens in. I would be accusing him without proof. And despite his powers, even Henri Joutel can't condemn a suspect on the word of someone who claims to be a witness. Plus I risk... *we* all risk incurring the wrath of the German or those he hangs around with. Not only would Marie-Élisabeth and the widowed Mrs. Talon suffer, but Mom, too!

Especially since the older Duhaut has found a way to come back to the fort to be with his brother. He claims he got lost while bringing up the rear of Mr. De La Salle's expedition. He says he had to stop to do up his hiking boots again and Moranget wouldn't wait for him. Henri Joutel reluctantly takes him back.

It doesn't take long for the Duhaut-Hiens trio to have the men challenging the authority of Mr. De La Salle's lieutenant. The fort reeks of conspiracy.

Harder than ever, I pray to God, my dad, and Armand, my dead brother, to help get us out of this situation. To repel the terrible men who continue to lay down their law, who attack Marie-Élisabeth—a good Christian—and who threaten my mom. But God, Dad, and Armand seem to have no intention of changing things. Or perhaps they're not able to.

I think I'll have to come up with a solution by myself.

"And what about my baby?" Barbier's wife asks for the millionth time, caressing a round belly that's close to giving up its contents. "Shouldn't my baby be laying claim to the seigneury promised by the king and not Talon's son, who was born on the ship, after all?"

Mr. Joutel often scratches his head, and not just because of the lice.

"Mr. De La Salle will decide upon his return. He shall determine which of the children has the right to the royal privileges."

When Barbier's wife cries out one night, rousing everyone in the fort from their beds, we discover that the matter will remain unresolved.

The child is stillborn.

Winter passes, the days alternating between mornings that cover the cactuses in frost and others when the sun brings out the insects. Every day, we wait in vain for news from Mr. De La Salle. To pass the time and keep minds occupied, Joutel has a more elaborate fort built for the men that at last resembles the first. But the deaths continue. De La Salle's lieutenant might not be as demanding as his master, but the climate is. Fever and pleurisy kill their share of settlers.

And then there's the Karankawa, who sometimes timidly try to attack our fort. Fortunately, powder and musket balls easily keep them at bay.

"Happy birthday, big guy!"

"It's my birthday?"

"You turned fourteen yesterday or the day before, I don't remember which."

While Isabelle Talon's sons shower me with friendly punches, she pecks me on the cheek.

"This time you really are a man," she says.

Perhaps she remembers that her husband told me exactly the same thing last year, word for word.

"Oh! Not for another year," Mom sobs. "He's still so young…"

Marie-Élisabeth doesn't share the ball of cake Mom made for me by skimping on our sugar rations for weeks. There's a little piece for everyone. Pierre and Jean-Baptiste don't think twice about wolfing down their sister's share. I don't even have time to stop them.

"And in a few days, Marie-Élisabeth will be…"

Twelve. Marrying age.

My heart races just thinking about it. Not with desire, but apprehension.

Are we ready to live our lives as adults?

∽

Springtime brings with it leaves on the trees… and Mr. De La Salle!

We're mightily relieved to be reunited with our expedition leader. His being there will at last cool hot tempers.

But, at the same time, how disappointed we are to hear that he still hasn't found the Mississippi!

"And *La Belle*?" he asks. "She's not moored opposite the fort?"

"Still wintering in the bay we chose, sir," Joutel replies. "The same men are guarding her as when you left."

"We shall use her to explore anew. By sea this time, staying close to the coast. I am convinced that we overcompensated for the currents pushing us east. We are too close to the land the Spanish call Texas."

"I share your opinion, sir."

With De La Salle back in Saint Louis, work picks up again until it reaches the frenzied pace our leader is renowned for. No doubt because he's obsessed with his thirst for discovery, because he's beginning to doubt his dreams for a colony, his orders become more and more demanding—and contradictory. One day, we build an emergency palisade because he's afraid of ever-greater numbers of Karankawa prowling around the fort; the next, we are to stop work on the palisade to dig an irrigation canal that is of no real importance.

One morning, three or four sailors who stayed behind on *La Belle* suddenly appear on a makeshift raft. They're a sorry sight: they have withered away to nothing and their clothes are in tatters.

"*La Belle* sank, sir," we learn from one of them. "All the men with us are dead."

"The Karankawa?" worries one of our leaders.

"No, sir. Thirst."

"Thirst?"

"We ran out of water. There was none nearby. We went ashore to look for some. We lost the rowboats. Then, off in the distance, we saw *La Belle* run aground and sink. Strong winds and an untimely current..."

The news spreads through the colony like a squall from the north. Without a boat, we are condemned to stay here, unable to find the blasted Mississippi or go back to France for more supplies.

"We'll do without," De La Salle eventually says. Despite his flaws, he takes even the nastiest surprises in his stride.

And so it is that in mid-April 1686, barely a month after he came back, he leaves again. This time, he takes twenty men with him, including his servants, his personal surgeon, his nephew Moranget, the younger Duhaut brother, L'Archevêque, and... Hiens!

Hiens!

Marie-Élisabeth is once more free from his hold.

A shame that the older Duhaut brother is still with us.

On the back of our hardships, there is mounting discontent among the settlers. Joutel has his work cut out maintaining order, even with the worst hotheads out of the way. He might be the only one of his faction left behind, but the older Duhaut brother doesn't stop speaking ill of Mr. De La Salle for a second. Even some of the Recollects can't help but write some awful things about our leader.

"There's a lot of misfortune in our colony, all right," I admit as I sit beside Marie-Élisabeth one night. She's keeping me company on my watch. "There's a great deal of danger. And then there's your dad. Ah, I mean..."

"I know what you mean, Stache. Dad's not with us any longer. Neither's yours. And my brothers are too young... You're the man to take care of us."

My head spins for a moment as she spells out the duty that falls to me. Not because I've only just become aware of it—I've been thinking about it for a long time now—but because now I know that Marie-Élisabeth knows, too. That she admits it. And that she's ready to put herself in my hands. Or at least I think she is.

Ever since Lucien Talon's death made me the oldest boy in our circle, Marie-Élisabeth has agreed that I'm now responsible for our families: my own and the family of the girl I will marry. Deep down, Mom must think the same. And Isabelle Talon, too.

I swell with pride inside. I tell myself that I'll have to show how worthy I am... especially if Marie-Élisabeth puts herself in my hands so willingly. I didn't think she would.

"Stache..."

"Yes, Marie-Élisabeth?"

I realize she's no longer watching the setting sun. Instead she's staring into my eyes. Does she want to kiss me? After a string of bad news, this would make for some rare good news.

"Stache," she says again, her eyes wet.

"Yes?"

"I'm pregnant."

28

ONCE BLUE

"Idleness breeds boredom and impatience," Henri Joutel sighs to a handful of trusted men. "Even threatening to hang the more excitable ones won't calm them down."

Our poor lieutenant, as he awaits news or the return of Mr. De La Salle, no longer knows how to occupy men who do nothing but hunt, fight among themselves, and speak ill of our expedition leader.

"Perhaps what we need is a good attack from the Indians to rally everyone together," says Barbier philosophically.

"Let's not speak of even greater disasters," Joutel counters. "Occupy the men by having them change the hide roofs on our buildings for bark ones." The hides, all dried out in the sun, have shrunk so much that several shelters are leaking like baskets with holes in the bottom.

"There are the women, too, sir," begins the marquis de La Sablonnière. "Even though the colony is not yet on its feet, I would like you to know of my interest in marrying the young girl of eighteen who is—"

"Out of the question!" Joutel replies, his expression making it clear that the matter is not up for discussion. "For the moment, the girls are sacred. Not to be touched. Not before there is a fort standing on the shores of the Mississippi. Only then will we proceed with nuptials."

"But what about Marie-Élisabeth and me?" I ask silently. "What will happen once everyone finds out she's expecting a baby out of wedlock? Will I be accused of sins of the flesh or will we have to turn Hiens in?"

Mom and her own mother don't know. But the pregnancy won't stay under wraps for long. Marie-Élisabeth's belly is growing rounder, her breasts are swelling...

God, Dad, Armand, help me! I am a man now, but I don't know what to do. And I used to think that adults had an answer to everything.

In August 1686, after four months away from us, Mr. De La Salle reappears to widespread relief.

"And the Mississippi, sir?" Joutel inquires.

"Still nothing."

"And the Illinois, the Indians you are familiar with from previous voyages?"

"We met no nation that speaks a language approaching theirs. It appears that we are further away from previously discovered lands than I thought."

It looks as though no good news can pass between our leaders. As usual, they no longer even get worked up over it.

Of the twenty men who left with our commander in April, only eight remain, including Moranget, Liotot, Jean L'Archevêque... and Hiens! Gaunt and exhausted, the explorers are nevertheless radiant, glad to be back. Moranget in particular is pleased to show off five horses with makeshift bridles, their saddlebags filled with seed, beans, and corn.

"We traded with the Cenis Indians for them," says De La Salle. "Brave warriors indeed, who can't wait to form alliances with us. They—"

"And my brother? Where's my brother?"

René-Robert Cavelier de La Salle peers haughtily at the older Duhaut brother, looking every bit the outraged nobleman who was not greeted properly. But the desperado barely notices.

"Where is Dominique? What happened to him? He was with you! Hiens! Do you know?"

Moranget replies, not Duhaut's uncle or the German.

"He asked to go back along with two other miserable weaklings. The delicate little souls were unable to keep up."

"But that was two months ago," De La Salle adds with a frown. "If they haven't come back, they must be lost."

"Or the Savages killed them," Moranget shrugs.

"My little brother?" says Duhaut, his voice higher now. "You—"

Then he turns to Moranget. He seems to despise him more than even De La Salle.

"You let my brother die?"

"He decided to leave the group. He brought it upon himself."

We're all gathered around the men who have just come back, listening carefully to their news, and so we all see Duhaut's hand move to the handle of his dagger. He withdraws it right away, but no one is fooled. We all understand.

As soon as he gets the chance, Duhaut will relieve his heart of the vengeful hatred that has just flooded it.

With Hiens, Liotot, and L'Archevêque now back with us, Pierre Duhaut's plans for insurgency are more feverish than ever. Especially since the only thing that seems to console him for the loss of his brother is his burning hatred for our leaders. And he worries me even more since he seems to be more interested in my mom with every passing day. It's not that he's courting her—he's not classy enough to do that— but instead he leers at her with lustful, indecent, lecherous intentions every time she crosses his line of sight. And it's not as if Mom is trying to seduce him. Her too-long, too-warm dresses tied up to the neck give no hint of any charms she might have. And she would never ever respond to Duhaut's advances.

"Those louts disgust me," she confides to Isabelle Talon one day in a whisper. "They eat like pigs, you can smell them for miles around, and they swear four times in the same sentence. They're a far cry from the perfect matches you promised me!"

"No one's more disappointed than I am, believe me. All we need is for one of them to become infatuated with us and we'll have one as a husband once the colony's up on its feet."

"I'd rather have a pig," Mom replies.

Their guffaws surprise the men around them. After all, we usually don't have much to laugh about.

Mr. De La Salle is telling anyone who will listen that a fourth and final expedition will leave once the heat of the summer is behind us. Most of the able-bodied settlers will be on it because we won't only be looking for the Mississippi, we'll be heading up to Canada for help, too.

"Let's hope we get it right this time," I let slip one night as I'm having supper near Mr. Joutel.

"If we are determined to establish French America in the heart of Spanish territory," the brave lieutenant replies, "our commander in chief has little choice but to swallow his pride and seek help from French settlements to the north."

As we wait for the expedition to leave, the Karankawa become more insistent outside the fort. We kill some of theirs, they kill some of ours, and Mr. De La Salle orders better palisades to be built. The common enemy Barbier had been hoping for brings everyone together, and the tension abates.

One evening, as she does sometimes, Marie-Élisabeth comes to meet me at the corner of the palisade where I'm on duty. Resting the heavy arquebus against the stake, I keep guard over the side looking out over the river. It's my favourite spot. From here, I can watch the countless species of birdlife along the shore. And crocodiles out hunting are a welcome distraction from the monotony of the otherwise tiresome watch.

Marie-Élisabeth looks a little pale, if you ask me. She keeps a hand pressed to her belly, its roundness seriously beginning to show beneath her dress. Very soon, she'll have to confess to being pregnant.

"Are you OK?"

"It hurts a little."

"You'll have to… we'll have to—"

"No."

She rests her head on my shoulder to watch an immaculately decorated ibis take flight. The white outline traces a graceful crescent above the water lilies.

"We'll have to tell your mom sometime, Marie-Élisabeth. And Mr. De La Salle. And…"

"They'll want to know who the father is. I can't turn Hiens in. He doesn't touch me anymore, just glares at me so that I know to stay quiet. Stache, I don't want Hiens or that hateful band of men he hangs around with to take it out on my mom or my brothers. Or even your mom. Have you forgotten the threats he made? I already suspect he might be behind Dad's disappearance."

I stop myself from screaming inside. The burden of the secret surrounding Lucien Talon's death is a heavy one for me to bear alone. But I must keep silent. The German's actions also strike fear into my stomach.

I plant a kiss on my friend's hair.

"We'll say that I'm the father of your child. We won't say a word about Hiens."

"The Recollects will send you to Hell, Mr. De La Salle might throw you in prison…"

"Too bad."

She doesn't say another word, and when my watch is over, we return to our shelters, hand in hand.

Tonight I dream. That hardly ever happens. I have forgotten the dream by the time I wake up, but it leaves a chalky taste in my mouth. I am still trying to remember the images that left at dawn when an inhuman cry pierces the morning silence.

I recognize Isabelle Talon's voice only once she shouts Marie-Élisabeth's name. I run over to the women's quarters, past dazed men trying to shake off sleep, their eyes still half closed.

Mom meets me at the door.

"No, Eustache. Don't go in. Don't go—"

I go around her without even stopping. Her hand grabs at the cloth of the back of my shirt, but I'm strong now: she can't hold me back.

I discover Isabelle Talon on her knees, sobbing hard beside her daughter's bed. The thin sheet that protects Marie-Élisabeth at night is drenched in blood. The baby she was carrying has killed her. From the inside. As though the German freebooter used the child to continue chipping away at us all from afar.

The wide, once blue eyes of my sweetheart have turned a little ashen as they stare up at an angle in the ceiling. Her mouth is set in a grimace of stifled terror, the final admission of the surprise that supplanted the pain of the hemorrhage that took her.

So that's what the stomach pains the previous night had signalled. Perhaps it had hurt more than she had wanted to admit.

Marie-Élisabeth died as she had lived.

Without disturbing a soul.

29

THE CRY OF THE WOLF

Isabelle Talon accepted her husband's disappearance gracefully, but the same can't be said for her daughter's death. For much of the day, she howls over Marie-Élisabeth's body like a baying wolf. Madeleine and young Ludovic hide in Mom's skirt—Mom is already carrying baby Robert in her arms—while Pierre and Jean-Baptiste hover in the background, stunned. The Recollects come in turn to the women's shelter, taking over from each other for prayers and words of comfort.

But it's no good. She remains inconsolable until Mr. De La Salle, worried about the effect her bawling is having on the morale of the troops, intervenes. From outside, I can only catch snatches of the conversation.

"Madame, the sorrow you feel… understandable, nevertheless… God often tests his… only appropriate… and our state of mind cannot… control yourself in order that…"

He suddenly falls silent—no doubt midsentence—and I hear the floor squeak beneath the sudden shuffle of shoes. I think to myself that Mrs. Talon has stood up—I hear the

distinct rustle of cloth as her skirt brushes against the bed—
then the sound of the timber at the entrance, then—

Isabelle Talon rushes out of the shelter, her eyes blinking
in the bright sunlight. For a second or two she seems to be
looking for something—or someone—then she sees her
children around my mom, then she sees me. It only takes
her a second to cover the five paces separating us... and to
slap me harder than I've ever been slapped!

"You little bastard! Marie-Élisabeth was pregnant! You
killed her!"

I'm so stunned by the blow that it blurs my vision. It
takes a moment before I can see the reactions around me.
Behind Isabelle Talon's furious scowl, I make out Mom's
shattered expression, the frightened looks of the children,
the amazement on the faces of Joutel and his first mates,
the dumbfounded priests, and the other settlers looking on
sternly. Only Duhaut and Liotot exchange vaguely sardonic
grins, amused at the entertainment provided by a mother's
sorrow. Jean L'Archevêque keeps his head down.

When the widowed Mrs. Talon collapses in tears at my
feet, I instinctively look around for Hiens. I'm surprised to
find him off to the side, frowning, his bottom lip trembling.
For an instant, I'm almost moved to pity, imagining him
touched by the woman's distress, by Marie-Élisabeth's
death, maybe even by the loss of his child.

But a second later I understand.

He's afraid he'll be linked to Marie-Élisabeth's pregnancy.

With the death of the girl I was hopelessly in love with, I
discover the true meaning of absence and dejection. When

my dad died, I had been too young to feel much; when my brother left us, it had been coming for a while. But Marie-Élisabeth! Blown out like a candle left beside an open window!

There had been no hint that she was about to leave us, aside from the throbbing pain in the stomach she had complained of the night before. The surprise of her passing only magnifies my misery.

Marie-Élisabeth. Secretive and unassuming Marie-Élisabeth, even when she had suffered most; the repeated rapes endured in silence, proof if ever it were needed. Placed by God on my path so that we might walk along together. All our lives. To accompany me, build our Louisiana with me, our little corner of France in America. Marie-Élisabeth. A demon has gulped down your existence, as though delighting in the blood of a sacrificial pig.

Marie-Élisabeth.

Alone in my corner, I move off to take my turn to cry, all day and all night long, then all the next day and all the following night. When I come back to accept my mother's wordless pardon—she assumes that I am the stillborn child's father—I have used up my reserves of grief. My heart is dry. Bone dry. All that remains inside of me is a violent urge to kill. A hatred and thirst for revenge too strong to be Christian. Too strong for me to avoid Hell if I let it guide my intentions.

But even the thought of the fires of Hell is not enough to divert me from this new course.

For weeks after Marie-Élisabeth's death, Isabelle Talon refuses to speak to or even acknowledge me. She doesn't answer my questions or respond to anything I say, even when it involves her children, whom I continue to treat as my own siblings. Her relationship with my mother, cold at the start, gradually returns to normal, with the occasional fit of the giggles. There's no longer much to laugh about in the colony, apart from certain evenings, when the usual drunks have too much brandy. But their guffaws bring no real joy to our miserable situation.

After many postponements, Mr. De La Salle's fourth voyage of exploration is at last planned for January. This time Mr. Joutel will be part of the expedition and Barbier will stay behind as governor at Fort Saint Louis. To defend us if ever the Karankawa attack, twenty other men will also stay behind with the women and children. For our survival, seventy-five pigs, twenty chickens, a few barrels of flour, musket powder, lead shot, and eight cannons but no cannon balls remain in reserve.

"Mrs. Talon, I would like to bring your son Pierre with us. It will be a weight off your shoulders and make him a man who's capable of looking after you and your children when he comes back."

Mr. De La Salle is holding his large feathered hat against his thigh. This exposes his terribly worn-out wig, making him look more like a churl than if he resigned himself to his natural hair, as he looks Marie-Élisabeth's mom straight in the eye.

"But he's only ten," she replies.

"As you please, ma'am. But Pierre could learn a great deal alongside Eustache."

"I will be helping look after the horses, Mrs. Talon," I chip in, interrupting as I wouldn't have dared just a short while ago.

I'm starting to feel more self-assured as an adult.

Isabelle Talon, just as she's done since her daughter died, pays no attention to what I say. But I know that deep inside she's not completely ignoring me because when Pierre says…

"Oh please, Mom! I'll be safe with Eustache."

…she tells Mr. De La Salle:

"Very well, sir. If my son is so enthusiastic…"

Then, sighing more than is necessary, she concludes:

"At least if the Indians breach the Saint Louis defences, there will still be a Talon alive."

Strangely enough, Mom also takes news of my departure calmly. Perhaps she imagines, just like her friend Isabelle, that the fort won't withstand a Karankawa attack. Perhaps she's resigned to dying. Or to the compromise of letting me escape an early grave by moving away from her.

When the time comes to go our separate ways, I can see the distress in her eyes—dejection not unlike the emotions she felt back when we were begging on the streets of La Rochelle—but at the same time I can see a glint of something she didn't have back then: dignity. My mom no longer has to grovel to live, despite the misery and death that hound us with relentlessly. She earns her daily pittance one thousand times over by working hard and putting her life on the line.

Plus, she's proud to be on an adventure that's bigger than us, bigger even than De La Salle. An adventure as big as life itself. Win or lose. She knows that by working hard to extol our faith and language, we are helping spread the immortal hopes of a nation worthy of its history.

PART V

The Final Expedition

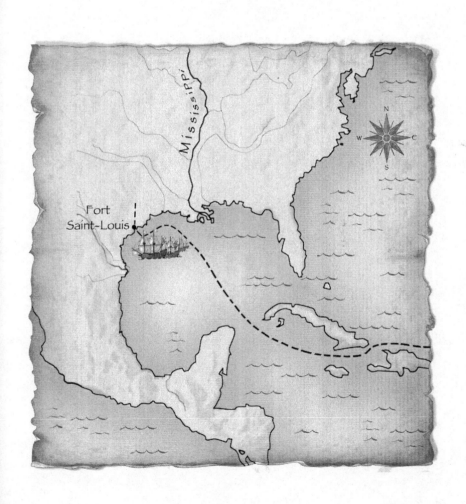

30

THE FINAL EXPEDITION

And so on January 12, 1687, I set off with Mr. De La Salle on the final expedition that will see us reach the mythical Mississippi and then on to Canada and Europe. Assisted by Pierre Talon, I'm in charge of two horses at the back of our group. Ahead of us, apart from our leader and his lackeys, are Henri Joutel, the Recollect priests, the older Duhaut brother, Jean L'Archevêque, Hiens, Liotot, and a few others. Moranget and a few men I barely know are bringing up the rear not far behind us.

For days, then weeks, we cross endless prairies, clusters of huge trees, lilting rivers, raging torrents, and lush, dense forests teeming with more birds and animals than I can count. Every day brings new surprises and marvels, making it easier for me to forget the two women I left behind: Mom... and Marie-Élisabeth. But their memory lives on with me, of course, and often when evening comes and I try to find sleep, I miss them. At the same time, these memories are a great comfort to Pierre Talon and me whenever our bodies hurt or are overcome with fatigue.

"Remember everything we find, Pierre. Memorize it all as best you can. One day, you'll have to describe all these wonders to your mom."

"Yes, Eustache. And... happy birthday, Eustache!"

"It's my birthday? How did you know?"

"Actually it's mine. I'm eleven. You turned fifteen... maybe three weeks ago now."

"Ha! So you wanted *me* to wish *you* happy birthday!"

I feel a twinge of sorrow. I'm sure that one month ago my mom made a cake to eat with my ghost. Thanks, Mom.

The Karankawa back at Fort Saint Louis proved a threat, but the Natives we meet along the way are incredibly friendly. There are so many nations that we have a hard time telling them apart. Only Mr. De La Salle and Joutel can manage it, and even then only by writing down their names.

"The Spichcets, Kabayes, Thecamons, Theauremets, Kiaboha, Chaumenés, Kouans..."

Each time we pass through a village, we are welcomed like lords. They ask us if we would like to eat and drink, give us supplies for the road ahead. Some of our men take the chance to slip off for a moment with their girls, some of whom join our group. Mr. De La Salle is only too happy to accept them.

The Natives say the same thing everywhere we go: they know other white men, like us, who come from the west and the southwest. White men who speak a language different to ours and who are incredibly violent. We are happy to learn that the Natives are all enemies of the Spanish from

Mexico and that they will gladly become our allies, especially since we have powder weapons.

To our surprise, in three different villages we meet Europeans who lost their way on past expeditions years earlier. A man called Ruter, a Breton, is one of them, with coarse manners and a weasel face. I'm not especially pleased to see him join our ranks. Particularly since the men fall in so quickly with the Duhaut-Hiens group.

There's also a man by the name of Jacques Grollet, who tearfully thanks Mr. De La Salle, and another named Meunier, who says he's from Provence. For several days, I doubt if he's ever set foot there: he can barely speak French and he's tattooed just like the tribe he lived with. But I come to see that poor old Meunier simply got lost a long, long time ago.

Despite the wonders and the friendly encounters along the way, tension continues to mount between the Duhaut and Moranget factions. Both men detest each other and take every chance they get to fuel their mutual hatred. It might be a barked order, or a blatant case of dishonesty; a favour granted to men close to De La Salle, or a reluctance to share the meat of a dead animal.

Mr. De La Salle turns a blind eye. Like any nobleman, he refuses to lower himself and get involved in quarrels between commoners, quarrels that are in his eyes petty squabbles over nothing. And when Mr. Joutel tries to play the peacemaker, our leader cracks the whip, calling out, "Henri, come here!" and going over his plans for the day with him.

The Natives observe these internal differences with a mixture of surprise and amusement. I think they imagined that we were somehow different, above such pettiness. But the entertainment makes up for their disappointment.

At last, in the spring of 1687, we finally reach the Cenis tribe that Mr. De La Salle encountered on his previous expedition. Keen to help us, they agree to guide us to the Mississippi Delta and meet the mysterious Illinois who are to escort us to Canada.

31

AS THOUGH HE KNEW

On March 15, 1687, our mood is as dull and grey as the sky. We are exhausted, and our food reserves have seriously diminished. Hunting hasn't met with much success over the past few weeks and we need to stop for a while to stock up again.

"We shall put the tents up here," Mr. De La Salle announces, pointing to the grassy plain around us. "I am familiar with this place. I came here on my previous journey. It is not buffalo season, but they can sometimes be seen where the land dips, further on. And last year, on the other side of the river, I left dried provisions I no longer had any use for. We had so many dead men..."

"Shall I send men for them, sir?" asks Henri Joutel.

But La Salle turns to two men who had been with him at that time, including one by the name of De Marle.

"Do you recall the cave? By the tall oak trees?"

"Of course, sir," De Marle replies.

"Take a few Indians with you and fetch the food there. And take these hotheads with you, too. They're always trying to pick a quarrel with Moranget. It will give them a break... and us a break from them."

"Very well, sir."

"You, Henri. You have a good eye. Go flush out an animal that's in fine health down below. Fresh meat will do us good."

Joutel glances at me before replying. I know that he's going to ask me to go with him to look after his arquebus and powder, but I'd rather not. I'd rather follow the others and stick close to Hiens. Even though I need no longer fear for Marie-Élisabeth, I have other projects concerning him.

"My musket needs cleaning, sir," Joutel finally admits. "It will blow up in my face. Give me a day, sir."

"Very well, Henri," Mr. De La Salle replies without hesitation. But he turns away as he says it, as though to express his annoyance.

As is his wont, in his little book Mr. Joutel jots down the names of those who go off looking for food this morning. Along with a dozen or so Natives, alongside De Marle and his companion who know where the food can be found, he writes the familiar names of Duhaut, Hiens, L'Archevêque, and Liotot. He adds Saget and Nika to the list, Mr. De La Salle's personal lackeys. The group finds a ford in the river and the men disappear one by one over to the other side like beads on a rosary.

The storm begins five minutes later.

It rains all evening and all night. We stay in our tents as much as possible, except when Pierre Talon and I have to take care of the horses. We tied them to the shelter under the branches of a longleaf pine. And on the morning of March 17 it's still pouring.

"The river looks set to swell up more than a butcher's belly," Henri Joutel mutters to himself, hands on hips as the rain runs off his hat and down his back.

So imagine our surprise when we see Saget, one of the servants sent off for food with the other men, appear on the other side of the river. He waves to us then wades across the ford. The water is up to his knees, and he's grinning from ear to ear.

"Well, lackey?" inquires Mr. De La Salle, barely giving the young man time to reach our shore. "What good news do you bring us? Did you find the provisions we hid?"

"No, sir. Well, yes, sir. But they had spoiled. All rotten."

De La Salle expected as much for his disappointment scarcely shows. The same can't be said for the men around us. But our leader realizes there must be a reason why Saget returned alone.

"Go on. Spit it out," he says.

"We ran into some buffalo on the way back. There must have been twenty of them. We managed to kill a few."

"How very—"

The rest of Mr. De La Salle's sentence is swallowed up by the men's shouts for joy. The thought of eating fresh meat fills them with enthusiasm. That much is clear.

"I will need a horse, sir," Saget explains. "To carry all the meat that the others are cutting up."

"With pleasure!" Henri Joutel cries, turning to me.

"Eustache, big lad. Can you put a packsaddle on the little mare?"

"Certainly, sir. I'll be ready to follow Saget in fifteen minutes."

"No," Mr. De La Salle interrupts. "It is Moranget who... Moranget! Where are you? Ah! There you are, nephew. The boy will prepare the animal and you shall go with Saget. Take another man with you, a strong one. Not a child."

I bite my tongue. If there is one person on this campaign who still hasn't noticed that I've become an adult then it's our leader. It's enough to make you think he remembers everyone's weak spot just to poke them from time to time. For no good reason. Just for the hurt it causes. I can see how, on top of all his obsessions, he has managed to raise everyone's heckles.

"And be quick about it, boy," Mr. De La Salle shouts, turning around. "The river continues to rise."

A quarter of an hour later, Moranget, Saget, and a Native (the burly individual they were after and who surely has four times more muscles than I do) begin to wade very carefully across the river. The mare quivers at the end of its harness.

We huddle in our tents for the rest of the day and wait.

And wait.

Night passes. Then the day and night of the eighteenth. Then the day and night of the nineteenth. The rain is so heavy, the river so high, that the noise drowns out all gas, burps, and snores. Living at such close quarters, being outside in the rain isn't always such a bad thing.

Moranget and the others still haven't reappeared. Mr. De La Salle is getting worried: I've caught him scanning the other shore each time I've gone outside to answer the call of nature or to take care of the horses.

AS THOUGH HE KNEW

The sky is at last dry on the morning of March 20. A timid sun tries to break through the clouds.

Down by the river, Pierre Talon and I are washing the pails belonging to Mr. De La Salle's cook. De La Salle himself is not far away, looking out at the water.

"Do you see that shrub from last night?" I ask Pierre. "The water level is down around its base. That shows it stopped raining upriver earlier. There's not much runoff water adding to it."

"No one on the opposite shore, sir?" Joutel inquires as he joins his superior.

De La Salle makes do with a shake of the head. His wig slides across his damp brow and he has to readjust it. In his other hand, he's holding his hat, still wet from the night before.

He seems to be very nervous.

"Let's hope nothing happened to them," Joutel sighs, mirroring our leader's concerns.

Again, De La Salle just nods. His felt hat slaps against his thigh and the fingers on his free hand twiddle frantically with the curls on his wig.

I see that a few of our men are secretly looking at him. It seems like I'm not the only one to be intrigued by the nervousness that seems to have taken hold of René-Robert Cavelier de La Salle this morning. He's more nervous than ever.

We often joke among ourselves about his odd tendency to sense danger for no reason, to see threats that rarely turn out to be real... But since dawn, in his nervous twitches and hesitations, we've seen more tension than usual.

Perhaps the bad weather of the past few days has worsened his fixations. Perhaps they can also be put down to the prolonged absence of his nephew Moranget, his lackey Saget, or his Savage Nika, three people he holds dear. I don't know.

What is he feeling? What is he so concerned about? It really seems as though the leader of our expedition can see something coming. Something that he alone can see...

32

CROSSING THE RIVER

The river is lower now, and Mr. De La Salle decides to go look for the men who have disappeared.

"You have not loaded your musket correctly, sir," Henri Joutel tells him.

I rush to offer my services.

"Please, let me, sir."

I take Mr. De La Salle's arquebus, place the powder required in the barrel, insert a medium-calibre musket ball (enough to kill a close enemy on the spot but not a distant animal), push down the wad, make sure the wick is nice and dry, then hand the weapon back to our leader.

He doesn't thank me. He ignores me, as usual. But perhaps this morning that's because of the worry that's gnawing away at him.

One of the Recollect priests steps forward. Contrary to common sense, the priests on our expedition insist on walking in their awful frocks—they're warm, heavy, and very awkward indeed in the swampland, meadows, brambles, and undergrowth.

"If it might reassure you, sir, I'm coming with you," he announces.

De La Salle nods. His face remains turned to the other shore, where only the tall grass of the plain can be seen. Still without saying a word, with a simple nod of the head he motions for a Native to come with him, too.

I'm still holding the boiled-leather flask containing the musket powder. I put a few of the balls in my pocket.

"I'll reload, if need be, sir."

De La Salle still doesn't answer. It's as though I don't exist. But I know that with his lackey gone he must be pleased to hear my offer. I take his silence to mean that he agrees.

I give Pierre Talon a quick wave goodbye and run off toward the river, following our leader, the Native, and the Recollect priest.

The waves are still high when we cross the ford. Twice I have to hold on to a rock to stop myself from falling into the water, and it's not easy keeping the powder dry. By the time we reach the other side, the spray has soaked us from head to toe.

We wade a little longer through the marsh, knee-deep in water. I hold the flask above my head and look all around. All we need now is for a deadly snake to bite me or— worse!—for a crocodile to go for my throat.

"Vultures!"

Mr. De La Salle's voice is a little unsteady. We're back on dry land and I'm busy emptying my buffalo-hide shoes of their leech soup.

"Something's happened," the priest replies.

Not far away, huge black birds are circling the plain and the edge of a scattered forest. But we have no way of seeing what they're flying over.

"The Savages?" the Recollect wonders aloud, worried.

"Perhaps," Mr. De La Salle replies, lighting the wick of his arquebus.

"Let's hope nothing happened to your nephew or—"

"We'll call them."

He raises his musket to his shoulder and fires into the air. The vultures briefly scatter at the sound.

"Allow me to reload, sir," I offer Mr. De La Salle.

But he has already walked off. He has recognized one of our men. Standing by a tree trunk, he's waving his arms at us. I've just realized who it is myself: it's Jean L'Archevêque.

"Praise God," the priest sighs.

Mr. De La Salle should be pleased too, but I can still see the nervousness in his every movement.

He can still see something coming.

"Your weapon, sir," I insist.

Either I needed to speak louder or his mind is elsewhere. Without paying any heed, he walks off slowly in L'Archevêque's direction. All his senses seem to be on alert: he keeps looking left, then right, then left again...

"Very well, Jean," Mr. De La Salle suddenly shouts at L'Archevêque. "So where is my nephew Moranget? Why has he not come to meet me?"

L'Archevêque, who also looks a little nervous, steps forward, clutching his musket.

"Moranget is adrift, sir!" he shouts.

De La Salle stops in his tracks.

"What do you mean, adrift? In the river?" he replies, his voice shaking.

"Yes, sir."

"Did he drown?"

By way of an answer, L'Archevêque bites his lower lip and looks our expedition leader in the eye. Right then, amidst the high grass, I see the reflection of an arquebus. It's pointed right at Mr. De La Salle's head.

33

MR. DE LA SALLE'S
PREMONITION

When I see the smoke begin to rise around the arquebus, instinct makes me close my eyes. I hear the sound of the detonation, new cries go up from the birds, then I open my eyes again.

Mr. De La Salle is still there, not far from me, but on his knees. For a fraction of a second, I think he's readying himself to beg the man who's to shoot him down for mercy, but then, suddenly, his wig slips off his head. Now I can see the wound on the side of his skull.

The leader of our expedition falls, face first. His last words were to express concern that his nephew Moranget had drowned.

Jean L'Archevêque runs a nervous hand across his face, then looks toward the man who opened fire. The man walks out of the grass he had been hiding in.

Pierre Duhaut!

"May our Lord Jesus Christ protect us!" gasps the Recollect priest.

The priest acts precisely how I expected Mr. De La Salle to, kneeling down to ask for grace. The Native man who came with us runs away. I'm rooted to the spot, unable to take in the drama that has just unfolded. It all seems too unreal: a merchant firing a musket ball at point-blank range into the head of a nobleman and the head of a mission into the bargain! It's practically treason. At the very least, a case for the hangman and gallows.

"Fear not, fear not!" L'Archevêque says, holding out a hand to the priest. "Duhaut, do not reload! You have nothing to fear, not from the reverend and not from Eustache. We will not harm you, Father, we swear. Nor you, big lad. We had no bone to pick with you. Our fight was with the leaders who despised us and—"

"With the kid, too!" Duhaut cuts in, stuffing his arquebus with powder without taking his eye off me for an instant. "That brat has been out to get us for too long now. He'll jump at the chance to turn us in."

"So what?" grumbles L'Archevêque, striding across the six paces that separate him from his partner in crime to snatch the musket out of his hands. "We agreed to get rid of Moranget and his uncle. That's done. The hostilities have ended. Kill Eustache and you'll have to do in all the others, too. They'll all be against us then. Every one of them'll be a potential snitch. As things stand now, most people approve of our handiwork."

He turns to the Recollect.

"Isn't that right, Father?"

"Yes... Yes, of course. We approve... I mean, we do not approve, but we do understand."

"And you, Eustache?"

I'm about to reply that not only do I not agree with their disgusting actions, but I'll be mounting a conspiracy the first chance I get. I don't have time to, though. Leaping out like a monkey, arms raised and legs bent, Liotot suddenly appears. His hair and beard are filthy, his appearance is nothing short of dishevelled, and his face is twisted into a sadistic, mocking grimace. He's chuckling to himself like the madmen who sometimes wander around outside the lunatic asylum back in La Rochelle.

"Look at the state of you, milord! You're less smart now, aren't you, milord?"

And he kicks away at Mr. De La Salle's lifeless figure, desecrating the body of a man who, if you ask me, is worth ten pathetic losers like Liotot.

"Take that! And that!"

Hiens appears in turn, glancing indifferently at the priest and me. For now, they're most concerned with plundering Mr. De La Salle's possessions. Just as viciously as Liotot before them, they forget about their humanity and any respect for a defeated adversary and take out their hatred on the body using their fists and feet. Next they undress him, one keeping his shirt, the other his pants, a third his shoes or hat, even the wig, in a share of the spoils that makes me want to spit in their faces.

Only De Marle stands back, shaking with fear and disgust. Clearly he doesn't approve.

The Natives who came with us watch the scene, their surprised amusement giving way to real horror. No doubt they're wondering what we might do to them, mere allies, if this is how we treat our leaders.

"Joutel's turn now!" Duhaut announces. "Time to get rid of another louse and anyone who tries to come to his aid."

He turns to me as he says this, almost hoping I'll step in.

"No!" says the priest. "Gentlemen, I implore you. Please do not further blacken your souls."

"Our souls are already stained, Father," says Hiens. "One less murder isn't going to spare us eternal damnation."

"Joutel is all right," L'Archevêque pleads, without looking at his companions, preferring instead to focus on the dagger they've just taken from De La Salle's personal effects. "He knows what's good for him. He knows he can't change a thing now."

"I'm not so sure," Liotot barks. "Not sure at all. I'd rather see him dead."

"Me too," spits Duhaut.

He stares at me hard with burning eyes before he goes on.

"And anyone who tries to get involved will get it too."

"And not just a musket ball to the head," adds Hiens. "That would be too quick, too gentle. A knife to the gut. That way he'll bleed for a long time. A *long* time."

We retrace our steps to find our way back to camp, but the rebels leave Mr. De La Salle's remains to the vultures and wild animals.

"What a sad end," I think. "The man might have had many flaws and obsessions, but he managed to overcome everything that stood in his way to leave France an empire right in the middle of Spanish America."

The life of an explorer can be just like the life of a widow: tough.

34

BACK AT CAMP

Back at camp, I'm relieved to see that Mr. Joutel is nowhere to be found. He left with two horses to let them graze. So he's safe from the murderers. De Marle, sitting at the entrance to his shelter, is trembling from head to toe, telling anyone who will listen what he just saw.

"We killed four buffalo and were smoking them, waiting for Moranget to come back with the horse to carry the meat to camp. We had set the marrowbone aside. We had eaten a lot, it's true, but there was plenty left. We found and killed the buffalo, after all. But Moranget lost it when he saw we hadn't waited for the others before eating. He said we were taking advantage of the situation to get more than our fair share. A fight broke out between him and Duhaut. So Duhaut, L'Archevêque, Hiens, and Liotot decided to kill Moranget, Saget, and Nika while they slept."

He is deathly pale and takes big swigs of brandy as he tries to find the courage to go on with his story.

"Liotot struck Moranget with an axe, then he cracked open the skulls of Saget and Nika. I couldn't speak I was so scared. Hiens, Duhaut, and L'Archevêque kept guard in

Natives tried to intervene. The lackeys died on the spot, but not the nephew. Moranget picked himself back up. There was blood everywhere. He kept opening his mouth to speak, but nothing intelligible came out. It was awful. I hadn't wanted any part of it and now I had to step in. 'Otherwise you might turn us in,' Hiens said. And Duhaut pushed a pistol into my hands. They made me fire. Moranget didn't make a sound between the axe falling and then the ball from the pistol hitting him. After that... after that..."

"After that, it's just like Eustache and I told you," the Recollect concludes, crossing himself. "They waited for Mr. De La Salle to arrive before slaying him, too. Then talk turned to ridding themselves of everyone close to our leader."

"They came back to kill us?" worries a fellow priest.

"No," De Marle replies, still shaking. "Only Mr. Joutel. They won't harm anyone who swears on the Bible to keep quiet about everything that's happened. They promise to spare those who agree to say our leaders were killed by the Indians, or taken by disease, or... anything at all, just not killed by their own men."

Instinctively, I glance over at the murderers. Pierre Duhaut, off to one side, is pretending not to look at us, while Liotot and Hiens are trying to reassure the Native guides. Several of them are threatening to leave the group: they never know what we're likely to do next.

"I don't see Jean L'Archevêque," one of the Recollects murmurs. "Could he already be off trying to kill Mr. Joutel?"

Suddenly worried, I leap to my feet and dash off to find the two men. It takes me no time to see them, walking towards us, side by side. Each is holding the bridle of the two horses Henri Joutel had led off to graze.

"There he is!" Duhaut shouts. "Death to the traitor working for the tyrant!"

And he whips out his pistol, running off in the direction of the two men.

"No, stop, Pierre! Stop!" Jean L'Archevêque shouts at him. "I explained the situation to Mr. Joutel. He understands. That's why he didn't run away. He's not armed and—"

Too late. Consumed by hatred, Duhaut pulls the trigger.

Click!

Saturated with humidity, the powder doesn't catch fire.

"Curses!"

The rebel hurls his pistol to the ground. He turns to Hiens, who is holding his arquebus.

"Kill him!" he orders.

"No, I said!" L'Archevêque shouts, moving in front of Joutel. "We've killed enough for now."

Hiens hesitates but doesn't lower the barrel of his musket.

"Mr. Joutel accepts all of our conditions," L'Archevêque insists. "He's a good officer... and we need him and his experience to find the Mississippi."

"I submit to your conditions," Joutel confirms. His voice is subdued, containing not even a hint of the fury I would have liked to hear from him.

Great men are easily won over, by the looks of things. Duhaut continues to work himself up.

"He'll betray us once we get to Canada. We'll be hanged or sent back to Europe, chained up in a ship's hold."

"Why go to Canada?" Hiens scoffs, with his usual disdain. "We can go back to Fort Saint Louis. We'll rebuild our lives there. There's everything we could wish for. Safety. Food. Even women..."

As he says it, he and Duhaut both look at me for a split second. Both are thinking the same thing. Pretty Delphine would make a tasty morsel. The widowed Mrs. Talon, too.

A wave of hatred rolls against my heart with such force that it leaves me dizzy. Then I feel better. I thank God for keeping the fire burning inside me that will fuel my ambition. If I had to quell my ill feelings and aversion toward the men behind the deaths of Lucien Talon and Marie-Élisabeth, I would no longer be able to live with myself.

My hatred for Duhaut and Hiens—for Hiens especially—keeps my heart and lungs working. Blood and air are keeping me alive. And where does life come from? From God.

Who said that God was against vengeance?

"God is against vengeance," objects a Recollect priest that same evening, while trying to calm those who remain faithful to our leaders. "Remember the message of peace brought by Jesus Christ. Only before their Creator can these murderers answer for their actions, only when they are judged at the brink of eternal life."

Joutel silently approves, his head lowered, ashamed at having given in to the rebels' demands, sorry for lacking the strength to stand up to their will, contrite at having been refused the only means of recovering a little of his dignity: avenging our leader's death.

"There's a certain fairness about how they have offered each of us the command in turn," the priest goes on. "That's showing repentance in a way, right there. They must already be regretting actions that were born of fleeting despair, passing anger. And having agreed to spare Mr. Joutel's life as well as our own shows there is goodness in them yet. Salvation, perhaps, for their damned souls. At any rate, we might manage to escape our fate, but they shall not."

The murderers are wary of letting anyone but themselves lead the group. And from what I've been able to overhear, Pierre Duhaut seems to be clinging to power as best he can.

"We'll take the Mississippi and reach friendly missions where we'll be safer."

"Safer?" Hiens exclaims, loud enough to be heard by people like me who are a good distance away. "In forts full of soldiers? Soldiers who might throw us in prison on the spot for having killed a nobleman in the service of the king?"

"A tyrant."

"What's the difference?"

Judging by the raised voices, the group's new leaders are already splitting into two clear factions. The harmony won't last long.

I thank God again for dividing my enemies. It makes my work easier, isolates the men I hate, and leaves them more vulnerable to my plans. All I need is a little helping hand and I'll be able to take care of the evil that I left Marie-Élisabeth open to, the evil that led to her death.

And God, once more, hears my prayer. It is answered a few days later. A tragedy opens the way for me to exact my revenge.

35

AMONG REBELS

De Marle and I are huddled under a horse examining an injury near its hoof when Hiens and Ruter, the Breton we found in the forest who quickly became his friend, walk past without seeing us. They talk away, not bothering to keep their voices down.

"There's no reasoning with the idiot," Hiens grumbles. "He's set on following Joutel to the Mississippi and up to Canada."

"It'll not be with me," Ruter replies. "I'm going back to the Savages. We've all the food we could want, all the women we could want, and we can live as free men."

"He'll never let us split up. He's raving mad. He'll kill us instead."

"Not if we kill him first," Ruter says, after a pause.

I bite down on my lip, not wanting to express how happy I am to see my enemies so divided. I look back up to see De Marle's crestfallen face.

"They don't know we heard them. We've nothing to fear," I murmur to calm him down once the two monsters are out of reach.

"But they... they're going to kill Duhaut. We have to warn him."

My sympathetic expression turns savage, like an animal.

"If you so much as open your mouth to let Duhaut know, I'll be the one who kills you in cold blood."

I'm no longer the shy little boy I was at the beginning of this adventure. I've become the worst, the most vicious of men.

I've lost track of the days, but I think it must already be early May. We zigzag from one makeshift camp to the next, without ever deciding whether to head north or south. Tensions mount among the rebels, while the others become more fearful. The Recollects calm everyone down as best they can, Henri Joutel dreams only of Canada... and I only of killing those responsible for my most recent troubles.

Most of us go to mass this morning. Pierre Talon is the altar boy. I saw Jean L'Archevêque go hunting earlier. These days he tends to keep his distance from the men he usually hangs around with.

Not far away, Duhaut and Liotot are pretending to take no interest in the ceremony. But I can see their thoughts are with the priests' prayers with every nod of their head. Perhaps they're beginning to worry more about their souls, sensing what lies ahead for them.

And they're not wrong.

The mass is coming to an end when Hiens suddenly bursts in. Ruter, Grollet, and twenty Natives are with him. Without paying us any attention, they march right over to...

"Duhaut, it's my turn to be in command," Hiens begins.

"As you like," Duhaut shrugs.

"And from now on we're heading south. Back to Fort Saint Louis."

Duhaut bristles at the news. Liotot, also nervous and as spiteful as usual, does the same.

"That's stupid. We're no match for the Karankawa."

"That's the way it is."

"It'll take two days, three, to take down the tents, pack up our supplies, load the horses..."

"We leave today. I'm the leader. You just said so."

"No."

Instead of showing annoyance, Hiens's features relax. As though he'd been hoping that's what he would say.

"Then we have a mutiny on our hands," he says, grabbing hold of the pistol on his belt.

He aims it at Duhaut's head. He's already pulled the trigger before Duhaut can react. The well-maintained wheel-lock produces the spark that lights the dry powder.

Duhaut's head explodes.

"My God!"

Liotot bends down to pick up the arquebus at his feet. But Ruter sees it coming. He moves more quickly, raising his own musket and firing. I can count three separate bloody stars that tear their way through Liotot's clothes. Ruter had loaded his weapon with more than one ball, by the looks of things.

His victim falls to the ground moaning.

"Good heavens! Good heavens!" chirrups a priest. "Are you going to kill us all?"

"Calm down, Sackcloth!" Hiens replies, his expression a mixture of irritation and sympathy. "No one else gets harmed."

He stares at Henri Joutel and me for a second.

"No one else," he repeats, reloading his pistol. "We need each other if we're going to make it out of this adventure alive."

"Apart from maybe L'Archevêque," says Ruter between gritted teeth. "We don't know which side he's on."

"The fact remains that you have murdered your comrade Duhaut in cold blood," retorts a Recollect, no doubt finding the courage to stand up to the killer because he's had enough of the murders.

"That's the man who killed our commander-in-chief, Father," Hiens answers. "I punished him for his crime, that's all. In exchange for this piece of justice, perhaps you might agree to plead in my favour if ever a new royal expedition comes to our rescue back at Fort Saint Louis."

Mr. Joutel rushes off to find Jean L'Archevêque to tell him what happened and let him know that Ruter and Hiens are out to kill him.

"But where can I run to?" the rebel wonders out loud. "I don't want to leave the group."

"I'll act as messenger," says Mr. Joutel. "I'll plead in your favour. Don't show yourself again until I've had them promise not to harm you."

Henri Joutel runs off to meet Hiens and Ruter.

"L'Archevêque will be more useful alive than dead," he argues. "The Caddo and the Cenis are our allies at the moment, but what happens if they turn against us like the Karankawa? There won't be enough of us white men to keep them at bay."

Given how the Natives now look at us with increasing distrust, the argument wins over the new leaders.

"Fine," says Ruter. "But we'll keep an eye on him."

And that's how Henri Joutel paid off his debt of honour to Jean L'Archevêque.

Duhaut died on the spot from a single ball, but Liotot, despite having been struck three times, continues to writhe on the ground. His slow death takes three hours. The Recollects have time to hear his confession and administer his last rites.

"My God! Will he ever stop moaning?" Ruter suddenly exclaims, putting his hands over his ears in a show of annoyance.

Hiens grunts in reply. Ruter picks up his arquebus and wordlessly stomps over to Liotot, who is still surrounded by the Recollect priests.

"Get out of there!" he shouts.

The priests step back in horror. The rebel puts the barrel of his weapon to the dying man's head and, without another word, fires one last ball.

The quarrel that divided the rebels is over.

"Pierre…"

Young Pierre Talon, convinced that I need a helping hand, hurries over to me. I'm a little ways from the camp, busy tying up the horses for the night.

"Pierre, you're no longer a child," I tell him, putting my arm around his shoulder. "You're eleven years old."

"You're right!" he replies proudly.

"Do you want to hear a secret? A terrible secret?"

He looks at me with Marie-Élisabeth's big blue eyes. His silence is the best consent I could wish for.

"Come on, then. Tonight I'll tell you something about how your dad and sister died."

36

THE RETURN
OF THE HUMMINGBIRD

Just like every morning, Hiens has gone off by himself to smoke his first pipe and let his thoughts wander. At today's camp, he's opted for a mound off to one side overlooking a stream. From behind a strange clump of pineapple trees and cactuses, he can keep an eye on the camp without anyone seeing him.

He uses orange leaves to sweep a few ants away from the base of a huge pecan tree. Leaning his back against the trunk, he lights his pipe, then, with the stem between his lips, gazes off into the blue smoke he blows out of his nostrils.

Pierre Talon was already hiding near the river before Hiens got there and the freebooter gives a start when he sees him.

"Was machst du dann hier?"

Often, when he speaks before thinking, his words come out in German.

Pierre acts surprised to see him—very well, if you ask me. I smile to myself as I think that Marie-Élisabeth's brother would probably be a hit with the other actors on the streets of La Rochelle.

"What are you doing here?" Hiens asks, switching from German.

He lets go of the pistol he had reached for instinctively.

"I came for a swim."

"You're disobeying orders? No one is to wander off from camp alone."

"I don't like taking my clothes off in front of everyone."

"You're afraid we'll laugh at your manhood? And what's this? What are you holding?"

"A green stone I found in the river. Do you think it's an emerald?"

I sneak out of my hideaway in the tall grass while Pierre distracts the German. I get closer, a heavy stone hanging from the end of my slingshot. I won't get a second chance. I need to get close enough to hit the target and hit it hard.

"*Das ist ein blöder Kieselstein.* It's only a pebble. It's not even green, only a little—"

The German whirls around to see me. I've barely got my slingshot going and he's already noticed the whir of the hummingbird. He's on his toes, all right! I suppose a man with his lifestyle has to be.

He loses all interest in Pierre, lets his pipe fall to the ground, and clutches the pistol pressed against his gut.

I don't have time to put more force into my shot or to aim any better. With the gasp of a leaping predator, the leather on my slingshot slackens and the projectile flies toward its target. Hiens uses his extraordinary reflexes to move his head out of the way.

The stone misses the temple I had been aiming for, hitting him above the eye. The blow doesn't have the impact I had hoped for and Hiens, instead of crumpling to the ground, continues to stagger backward, regains his balance, then draws his pistol and points it in my direction.

"*God. Damn. It.*"

Thankfully for me, his eyebrow has been cut and blood is pouring into his eyes. He's firing blind. I use the extra fraction of a second I've been given to hurl myself to the side. I've moved a foot when the gun goes off. The ball rips away part of my shirt sleeve, but I throw myself at Hiens without a scratch on me.

When Hiens wipes some of the blood away from his eyes with the back of his hand, he only has eyes for me. He's lost all interest in Pierre. Probably because he thinks he's too young. But Pierre has just picked up a club we left in the grass earlier. The hit that lands on our foe's shoulder isn't especially strong, but the element of surprise helps rattle Hiens.

The freebooter twists away and raises his elbow to shrug off the blow, allowing me to reach him. Our chests come together. My weight and momentum throw him off balance. He falls backward. I put my left arm around his neck and pull him tight. We collapse into the pineapples and cactuses. My shirt and pants are torn, my skin is cut to shreds, but I barely notice.

"Remember Marie-Élisabeth, you monster. And remember her father."

He grits his teeth, but I detect a hint of cheer in his anger. He must think I'm sure I have him beaten when he knows he's ten time times stronger than I am. He's thinking that in a second, maybe two, long enough to have some fun, he'll flip me onto my back and beat my windpipe to a pulp. He doesn't even think to pin my free arm, which could swing a hook at him. Blinded by blood, he doesn't see a thing coming.

My right shoulder tightens and my fist comes down. It's clutching the knife with the broken handle used to kill Lucien Talon. Hiens takes the blade right in the chest, spluttering more with surprise than pain. He grabs at the back of my shirt while his free hand searches frantically for my wrist. But this time I go for his gut. His hands go straight to the wound and I attack his chest again.

I don't think I got the heart because he's still clawing at my clothes. Giving everything he has, he manages to grab the wrist I'm holding the knife in.

"I'm not the one stabbing you, you monster," I gasp. "It's Lucien Talon. With the same knife that killed him."

I've ground to a halt on top of him. With nothing but contempt to throw at him. And I don't hold back.

"And Marie-Élisabeth. You like raping little girls, don't you? She's happy now too. She's smiling down at us from heaven. But you'll be burning in hell. And the day I tell my mom all about this morning, she'll burst out laughing and spit on your memory."

Still blinded by the clumps of red spattered across the whole top half of his face, he opens his mouth to reply. Will he ask forgiveness for his sins? Or respond to my hatred with a fury approaching my own? I'll never know. Bubbling scarlet floods his mouth and spills out over his beard. His lungs have been punctured. His chest rises in one final effort to pull in air... and falls down flat for the last time as he drowns in his own blood.

The seconds tick by slowly as his fingers refuse to let go of me. In the end, I need Pierre Talon's help to dislodge them. Once I'm back on my feet, my gaze shifts back and forth between Hiens's body and the knife I'm still holding.

"The others are coming," Pierre says matter-of-factly, as though to keep his distance from the horror he's just been involved in. "The shot must have sounded the alarm."

Between the stems of the cactuses and pineapple trees, I can make out a handful of Natives standing around Ruter, Joutel, and L'Archevêque. Arquebuses in hand, they advance slowly, looking all around them, afraid they'll come across the foes who surprised Hiens.

When they draw level with us, Joutel gasps in disgust and horror. I think he's less disturbed to see Hiens's body than he is to discover the perpetrators: two young members of the group, among the most mild-mannered and the most reserved of the lot.

"Well, well. How did you catch him out?" is all a surprised Ruter manages to say.

Strangely, no one seems sad to see the back of the German freebooter. No one even steps in when Pierre and I stand over the body to push it down the slope and into the stream. No one except for Henri Joutel.

"No. We have to... We have to dig a grave, give the man a Christian burial," he stammers.

I let out a roar of such hatred that it surprises even me.

"Did he let us do the same for Lucien Talon before he threw his body to the crocodiles?"

"Lu... Lucien Talon?" says Joutel in amazement.

"So it was Hiens that killed him," L'Archevêque wonders, but doesn't expect an answer.

"And when he was with Duhaut," I add, "did you give Mr. De La Salle a Christian burial? Or did you leave him for the vultures?"

Silence is my only answer.

"And you all knew about Marie-Élisabeth! You can't not have seen him forcing her to meet with him over all those years! He raped her for years. And no one came to her defence... or to mine when people said I was the father of her child!"

L'Archevêque pretends to be lost in thought. The Natives look on in amazement, many shaking their heads. Ruter looks at my torn clothing and bloody scratches with new-found respect.

"And all the trouble we had with the Karankawa! It all started because of him, because he went around murdering them! That meant he could put pressure on Marie-Élisabeth, show her the threats against her dad were real. He wanted her to see that killing meant nothing to him."

"The dead Savages? That was him?"

Henri Joutel seems completely taken aback.

"Hiens almost wiped out the whole colony just because he couldn't keep his hands to himself."

De La Salle's lieutenant goes from being dumbstruck to looking at Hiens with tears in his eyes. He's not crying for the German, far from it, but perhaps for Marie-Élisabeth and her dad. Maybe he's upset he didn't realize that the dangers facing the colony came from a single man. At the start, at least. Or maybe simply because he wasn't able to stop hatred and resentment from flooding the hearts of the two young men on his expedition.

"I won't write any of this down," Joutel says suddenly in a whisper. "This didn't happen. May everyone keep to himself the aberration that led these boys to take such drastic action. The harm caused by Hiens was such that they... they...”

An unconvincing, ill-timed laugh interrupts him. Everyone turns to Ruter.

“Well, boys?” he asks. “This the first time you killed a man? How do you feel? Any regrets?”

His second guffaw rings even more hollow. Joutel and L'Archevêque try to hide their disgust. I fling Hiens's knife to the ground, put my arm around Pierre's shoulder, and lead him back to camp with me. Without looking up, I reply: “Killing a demon who raped a little girl again and again for years doesn't leave you with any regrets. It's like slitting a pig's throat.”

37

THE VENGEFUL GOD

The God of the Bible is not the God of love and forgiveness proclaimed by the Recollects. He is a vengeful, violent God. Didn't He drown all of humanity, sparing only Noah's family, all because of a grudge? That's why He soothes me whenever I act just like He himself would have done.

Since I killed Hiens, avenging Marie-Élisabeth and her dad, I've felt good. Calm.

Happy.

Now, to improve upon the moments of peace that wash my soul, all that remains is for me to return to Fort Saint Louis. For Pierre and me to be reunited with our families. Once Pierre tells his mom why I couldn't speak out, once he tells her about our revenge, she'll forgive me for everything and we'll be able to live together just like before: with Mom, in harmony, happy just to be together. We'll be siblings again, and hold dear the memories of those we loved so much.

A few days after we killed Hiens—still in May 1687—Henri Joutel, the Recollects, and De Marle left with six horses and three Native guides in search of the Mississippi. After that, God willing, they'll travel on up to Canada.

"You can't go back to Saint Louis by yourselves," L'Archevêque worries as he chats to Pierre and me one evening.

"We'll ask the Native guides."

"The warm season is almost upon us. The buffalo will cover the plains. They'll be off hunting."

"We'll wait for them."

And that's how the first few months go by: living with the Caddo along with L'Archevêque and two other white men. To our great relief, Ruter—whom we have little in common with—goes off to live with another tribe much further west.

We quickly grow fond of the Natives and, even though we miss our families, Pierre and I decide to stay a while longer. Summer and fall pass so quickly, and winter is so cold, that we again put off our plans to leave.

"Happy birthday, Eustache."

"It's my birthday? My God! You're right. I'm sixteen."

Using the marks L'Archevêque scratches into a piece of wood, I conclude that it is indeed February 1688. I suddenly miss my mom.

"We'll leave in March."

But summer comes and we're still there. And it must be said that the Natives become aggressive every time we mention leaving. We no longer seem to be entirely masters of our own destiny. It's no real hardship: we're enjoying our life of hunting and fishing, reaping and sowing. We're learning how to live like Natives and we're sure that the knowledge and skills we pick up will be a big help to our own people, once we're back at Fort Saint Louis.

At last, using a hunting trip as an excuse, Pierre and I manage to sneak away from the families that welcomed us once the first cold of fall 1688 sets in. L'Archevêque and the others do not come with us.

And so we walk back the way we came. We retrace the steps taken by René-Robert Cavelier de La Salle, back when he still harboured outrageous dreams of rebuilding a little piece of France in the Americas.

We spend more than three months exploring each region we pass through, just like Mr. De La Salle would have done. We want to make the most of the plains and forests around Saint Louis in case we decide to move there later. We also become friendly with the Natives who live there.

Especially since we might need protection from an enemy common to all: the Spanish!

Talk turns to them everywhere we go. They are an increasingly common sight on these lands, and a source of preoccupation for the Natives. Some say the Mexicans have even learned that we're here. That they're looking for us.

Reason enough, then, to complete the last leg of our journey as quickly as we can.

We reach Fort Saint Louis in early January 1689. It appears in the distance, in the swirl of a damp morning.

Pierre and I would have liked to spend Christmas with our own, but we had to take a long detour. We skirted around Karankawa territory because, we were told, they had become increasingly hostile to our being on their land. Perhaps they have ties to the Spanish. Perhaps they're still bitter about the murders that happened when we were there—a wave of murders that Hiens started, needless to say.

"Oh my God! My God, no!"

I've come to a halt, just as we're about to walk down a hill that gives us an excellent view of the camp below.

"What is it?" Pierre asks, unable as ever to see much from a distance.

"The buildings. They've been... burned."

"You're... you're sure? We're still so far away."

For a moment I wonder why there are no signs of life. No smoke from a fire, no flag flying from the pole by the entrance, no one out fishing on the shore...

"Pierre! Fort Saint Louis has been destroyed!"

We find a small boat on our side of the river, half eaten by worms. We launch it without thinking twice. Short of breath, our hearts beating wildly, we paddle to the far shore—bailing the water out with an old hat for the last quarter of the crossing. The extent of the damage is clear as soon as we reach the first buildings.

The wooden stakes and buildings haven't burned to the ground, but they've been left unusable. The lean-tos are in pieces, the sleeping quarters have been gutted and exposed to the foul weather, the—

"Mom! Mo-om!"

Pierre Talon's shouting shatters my eardrums. I give a start, lifting a hand to my ears. Young Pierre runs over to a nearby body, sprawled on the ground. And the body is wearing a dress we've often seen on his mom.

Only then do I notice the other bodies. They're scattered across the camp, indicating that our people fled in all directions to escape the massacre. Broken arrows and spears, even a flint knife left behind after the plundering—it all points to an attack by the Natives.

"Not the Spanish," I mutter to myself, as though that were reason to be happy.

As I step around Pierre, now collapsed on the ground and weeping over his mom's body, I look for Mom. It doesn't take me long. She never did stray very far from her friend Isabelle.

Blood stains her clothes beneath her left breast. The arrow that hit her right in the heart had been recovered by her attacker. At least she must have died right away; she didn't have to suffer.

At first I look at her with detachment. It's difficult to think that the wax-like face, the eyes pecked out by birds, and the crumpled cheekbones once belonged to my mom. The body looks nothing like her.

And the stench!

I presume the attack came a few days ago. Or maybe weeks, I don't know.

Suddenly I think back to the vengeful God in the Bible. Why did he allow a massacre this time? To good Christians, too. Not even to monsters like Hiens or ungodly Savages!

Might it be to punish Pierre and me for killing the German? For not having done as the Recollects suggested? For not having respected the message of love brought by Jesus Christ? For having taken our revenge right when we thought we were pleasing God?

Religion is complicated!

"Eustache..."

It sounds like Pierre Talon has stopped crying. I don't turn around. I stay there, lost in my thoughts over my mom's body.

"Eustache..."

"What?"

"The Indians."

I stand up straight. Pierre is standing, too. Facing a clump of shrubs that mark a corner of the garden. Everything is rotten, I notice, overrun with prickly undergrowth and creeping vines.

I also notice, dead ahead, the dozen or so Karankawa staring at us, looking angry and clutching their weapons.

WHAT HAPPENED NEXT

Historians confirm that Henri Joutel and his companions reached the French outposts along the Arkansas River in the fall of 1687. They kept the circumstances surrounding René-Robert Cavelier de La Salle's death a secret and continued on up to Québec. From there, Joutel and the Recollects set sail for France at the end of summer 1688. They reached La Rochelle in October.

Upon their arrival, they learned that Captain Beaujeu's return and his report on De La Salle's expedition had greatly displeased Louis XIV. To such an extent that the king had forgotten all about Louisiana for a time. Years would go by before Pierre LeMoyne d'Iberville finally founded the French land dreamed of by De La Salle on the lands claimed by the Spanish.

In spring 1689, several months after the massacre at Saint Louis carried out by the Karankawa, Spanish troops led by Alonso de León found the French post they had been searching for since 1686. A man by the name of Jean Géry, lifted earlier from a neighbouring tribe, served as their guide. The Spanish took the youngest three Talon children from the Karankawa, who had been spared during the attack on Fort Saint Louis. The youngest two boys no longer even spoke

French. Their faces and bodies had been tattooed in the style of the Natives.

In 1689, Jean L'Archevêque and Jacques Grollet, tired of living among the Caddo, wrote a message that they entrusted to Natives allied with the Spanish. Alonso de León came to save them. The two Frenchmen remained prisoners of the Spanish for thirty months before serving in the Army of New Spain. L'Archevêque went on to marry twice, had children, and bought a property in Santa Fe. After an eventful life, he died in 1720, at a relatively old age, at the hands of the Pawnee.

ABOUT THE HISTORICAL CHARACTERS

The Talon family really did exist. The fate of each, recounted here, is true to the facts... aside from a detail or two that helped the novel along. For instance, young Lucien Talon, who shared his father's name, was renamed Ludovic to avoid confusion.

Lucien Talon Senior did indeed disappear in mysterious circumstances in fall 1685. No one knows what became of him. Marie-Élisabeth did indeed die at the age of 12... but from an unknown illness. Fatal, contagious diseases were rife at the time.

All those involved in the drama surrounding De La Salle's murder also really existed. Details of the ambush are true to historical events, as was the rivalry that led the rebels to start killing each other. I described them here using Henri Joutel's account—his travel diary was my main source of information. Like most historians, I consider De La Salle's lieutenant's account to be the most plausible of those to have reached us.

We do not know what happened to Hiens. Did the German freebooter live and die with the Natives? We don't know. I completely made up his murder by the two young men on the expedition.

History also lost all trace of Pierre Talon once Joutel left. No doubt the Caddo or the Cenis adopted him. It's unlikely that he tried to return to Fort Saint Louis, even accompanied by an older friend. Meanwhile, Jean-Baptiste Talon was found by the Spanish in 1691. The young boy was living with a nation that had possibly been given him by the Karankawa. A certain Eustache Bréman was freed along with him.

Also from Baraka Books

YA Fiction

The Adventures of Radisson
1 – Hell Never Burns
2 – Back to the New World
3 – The Incredible Escape
Martin Fournier

Break Away 1 – Jessie on My Mind
Break Away 2 – Power Forward
Sylvain Hotte

Adult Fiction

Speak to Me in Indian
David Gidmark

A Beckoning War
Matthew Murphy

The Nickel Range Trilogy
1 – The Raids
2 – The Insatiable Maw
Mick Lowe

History

A People's History of Quebec
Jacques Lacoursière & Robin Philpot

The History of Montréal
The Story of a Great North American City
Paul-André Linteau

*Soldiers for Sale, German "Merceneries" with the British
in Canada During the American Revolution*
Jean-Pierre Wilhelmy

Journey to the Heart of the First Peoples Collections
Musées de la civilisation
Marie-Paule Robitaille

Printed in March 2016
by Gauvin Press,
Gatineau, Québec